THE BUDDHA
Reveals

His Love and Enlightenment

THE BUDDHA
Reveals

His Love and Enlightenment

Dr. Varish Panigrahi

BLACK EAGLE BOOKS
Dublin, USA | Bhubaneswar, India

Black Eagle Books
USA address:
7464 Wisdom Lane
Dublin, OH 43016

India address:
E/312, Trident Galaxy, Kalinga Nagar,
Bhubaneswar-751003, Odisha, India

E-mail: info@blackeaglebooks.org
Website: www.blackeaglebooks.org

First International Edition Published by
Black Eagle Books, 2024

THE BUDDHA REVEALS
by **Dr. Varish Panigrahi**

Copyright © Dr. Varish Panigrahi

Cover & Interior Design: Ezy's Publication

ISBN- 978-1-64560-599-7 (Paperback)
Library of Congress Control Number: 2024949362

Printed in the United States of America

DEDICATION

This biographical story of Siddhartha Gautama Buddha is dedicated to the spirit of all the Buddhist philosophers and teachers who toiled to define and create a better world and spread the Dharma, but are mostly forgotten today:

Ashwaghosha
Nagarjuna
Asanga
Vasubandhu
Dignaga
Dharmakirti
Indrabhuti
Santarakshita
Padmasambhava
Lakshminkara
and many others.

- Varish Panigrahi

CONTENTS

Appendices

A: Map of Tathagata's World
B: States and their cities, 6th Century BCE India
C: Main Characters and Their Relationship
D: Schedule of Main Events in Buddha's Life
E: List of Vowel and Consonant Characters
F: List of Complex Consonant Characters
G: List of the Main Buddhist Sects
H: List of Books for Further Reading

Glossary

List of Illustrations

1. Tathagata and Yashodhara at the Birthday Party
2. Tathagata and Yashodhara at River Rohini
3. Yashodhara garlands Tathagata
4. Tathagata bidding goodbye to Channa
5. Tathagata giving Instructions to Five Disciples
6. Tathagata and Disciple in Yashodhara's Room
7. Tathagata in Maha Parinirvana at Kusinara

Preface

During my years of exposure to Buddhism in India and the United States, I realized that there was a need to bring out a more humane story of the Buddha so that everyone could get a realistic perspective of one of the greatest souls to walk on this earth.

A large number of anomalies and false images are widely prevalent regarding the life story of the Buddha. Popularly known life stories of Gautama Buddha have many inaccuracies that are inserted to accentuate his religious image. For example, it is presumed that Siddhartha Gautama left home as a monk on the day of Rahula's birth and not when Rahula was at least one year old. It is also generally not known that Rahula was accepted into Buddha's religious organization when he was barely eight years old and that Buddha ensured Rahula was given proper education and guidance during his childhood. Similarly, it is popularly not known that Buddha's aunt Prajapati and Yashodhara became members of the Bhikshuni Sangha started by the Buddha. Both of them eventually attained nirvana while they lived there. Buddha's half-brother Nanda and some of his cousins, Ananda, Anirudha, and Devadatta also joined the Sangha. Thus, Buddha had attracted most of his immediate family members to travel the road that he had chosen. It was Buddha's message that showed the way and removed suffering from thousands of followers including many of the citizens of Kapilvastu and the nearby areas. The Buddha carried out the responsibilities towards his family and friends even after his enlightenment.

Siddhartha and Yashodhara were cousins to each other. Hence, there was close understanding and stability in the relationship between them. It was natural for Yashodhara to sacrifice for the sake of Siddhartha and the family. The deep understanding between Siddhartha and Yashodhara was the prime force that enabled Siddhartha to set himself free from Samsara and strive towards enlightenment for the sake of humanity. Yashodhara's continuing support of Siddhartha's cause, even after his leaving home, and her eventual joining the Bhikshuni Sangha shows how she was in complete harmony with the Buddha's path. Hence, it could be truly said that a major force behind Buddha's ultimate success was Yashodhara's love and harmonious relationship with him.

This story of Siddhartha and Yashodhara, their romantic marriage and life as husband and wife, the birth of Rahula, and the eventual transformation in their relationship, needed to be told so that one treats them as mortals of flesh and emotions in an immortal partnership of love, understanding, and compassion. Their story is very relevant in today's world of selfishness, greed, and violence at every level of life. Parents and children should be told that Siddhartha did not abdicate his responsibilities when he embarked on a mission for the sake of humanity. He had made sure that his wife and the child were well taken care of at his parental house.

The life of Gautama Buddha depicted here is mostly

based upon the facts and characters found in the historical sources and the scriptures, except for some of the details in the early parts of his life. The author has filled up the gaps in the documented story of his early years, especially the details of his romance with Yashodhara and his eventual abdication of the householder's life.

The Buddha had a long life of about eighty years and he preached the Dharma incessantly for almost forty-five years after his enlightenment at Uruvilva. During this period, he maintained a close relationship with Bimbisara, the King of Magadha, and Prasenjit, the King of Kosala. Both of these contemporaries of the Buddha had tragic deaths towards the end of Buddha's life. These stories are also covered here along with a short history of the spread of the Dharma after the death of the Buddha at present Kushinagar. Since it summarizes in very few pages the events over a period of twenty-five hundred years and all across the world, it should be only taken as a pointer to more detailed accounts outside this book. In an Epilogue at the end of this book, the Buddha comes back to the present world to give his views on the state of the Dharma in the present world! Thus, this book covers the story of the Buddha's entire life along with the main tenets behind the Dharma he preached and the spread of the Dharma after him.

Whenever there was any occasion to talk about himself, the Buddha always referred to himself as 'Tathagata', the one who came as such. This story of Buddha is revealed through Tathagata as the narrator and hence it can be called Tathagata's story.

My travels throughout India, especially to Bodh-gaya, Nalanda, Rajgir, Sarnath, Varanasi, and other places associated with the Buddha and his relics, have helped me to better appreciate the central ethos running throughout the Buddha's life. One has to walk on the Sujata bridge over the river Niranjana to the main temple in Bodhgaya during a moonlit evening, to feel the walk that Siddhartha Gautama took for years during his awakening process! The Sarnath Park still has the same serene atmosphere as when the Buddha delivered his first message to his first five disciples. Lumbini Gardens, the birthplace of the Buddha, and Kushinagar, his final resting place, similarly reverberate with Buddha's messages of love and compassion for the whole world.

To maintain consistency, I have used the Sanskrit versions of the names and religious words rather than the Pali versions, especially since the more numerous Mahayana sects use the Sanskrit versions and most people in India are more familiar with them. An approximate map of the Buddha's world prepared by me is illustrated in Appendix A and it shows the location of the states and the cities and towns at that time. A list of these states and their capital cities and towns is shown in Appendix B. A chart in Appendix C shows the relationship between the main characters in the book. A schedule of main events in Buddha's life is shown in Appendix D. Appendix E shows the list of vowel and consonant scripts similar to what the Buddha would have used. Appendix F shows the list of complex consonant characters. Appendix G has a list of the main Buddhist sects that evolved in the different countries of the world. Appendix H has a list of books for further reading on the life of the Buddha, his messages, and the Buddhist sects. A glossary of the special words used in the book, most of them in Sanskrit, is given at the end.

During the writing of this book, many persons have helped and encouraged me. My wife Anuradha and son Arun provided support during the long periods when I was immersed in the writing of this story intermittently between my travels through India and the United States. I thank all the members of KalingaZEN Advaita Mahasangha, especially Brig. Niranjan Dhal and Sashi Bhushan Rath, for their friendship and encouragement during the project. Special thanks are also due to Shashi Bhushan Rath for his comments and suggestions on the final manuscript. I thank very well-known artist Rabindra Kumar Maharana for drawing the illustrations of the events in the Buddha's life in the traditional Odishan style.

I am especially indebted to Satya Pattanaik and Ashok Parida of Black Eagle Books for their attention and support for the production of this book.

Dr. Varish Panigrahi

President, KalingaZEN Advaita Mahasangha,
N3-B6, IRC Village, Nayapalli, Bhubaneswar, India
drvpanigrahi@aol.com, Mob: 91-9437506237

-1-

Birthday Celebrations

Tathagata was born in 563 BCE as Siddhartha Gautama, the son of Raja Suddhodana and Queen Maya of the Himalayan kingdom of Kapilvastu. Tathagata is telling his own story today, because all the stories that have been circulated about him depicted him as someone who was more sanctimonious than all the gods, whereas, Tathagata was only a mortal of flesh and blood with all the emotions of love and happiness like every one of you. Tathagata also lived the life of a householder until he was twenty-nine years old and he deeply loved his wife Yashodhara, his son Rahula, and his parents and relatives. After Tathagata became a monk, these relationships were transformed to a higher level, and their welfare was always of concern to him. But these aspects of his life story have not been generally presented to make him more of a god. Tathagata wants you to know him as the mortal man of love and emotions, as he was before he left home, and as the awakened one, who very much lived as part of this *Samsara* with love and compassion for every being.

The earliest recollections from his childhood are the celebrations when he was five years old. It was *Vaisakha Poornima* – the full moon day of summer. The palace of his father Raja Suddhodana at Kapilvastu was decorated with lights for the birthday celebrations in honor of him. Tathagata remembers that his father's sister Queen Pamita of Devadaha was there for the occasion, accompanied by her daughter Yashodhara. She was almost five years old then. Though he had heard about her from his parents, this was the first time he saw her. He thought then that she was a very cute and beautiful cousin of his. She was so full of spirits and played with him during the whole day just before the birthday celebrations. Her captivating smile and piercing eyes were so inviting that he became her friend then and there. Little did he realize then that this would be the most important relationship of his life.

On the full moon day, he got up very early in the morning and went to the palace temple for the religious ceremonies in observance of the birthday. His parents were there along with Queen Pamita and Yashodhara. He sat down in front of the deity, and the Brahman priest recited a few hymns in Sanskrit to bless him. His parents then blessed him and threw the sanctified flowers and rice grains on his head; Queen Pamita and other elders from the royal family also blessed him. They all then joined in a small feast that was arranged in the palace gardens. A group of about twenty children of his age had been invited to participate in these celebrations. After the meals, they played different games of running and jumping, musical chairs, hide and seek, etc. They dispersed at noon to go home and rest.

He got a chance to play again with Yashodhara in the afternoon. They played hide and seek within the palace building. The palace was lighted in the evening and musical events were arranged on the open-air stage in the palace gardens. He was especially enchanted by the playing of the flutes and decided to learn and play the flute one day!

Once the evening celebrations were over, Tathagata had dinner with his extended royal family at the palace banquet hall. Yashodhara and Queen Pamita were also there. Tathagata's father said, "Siddhartha, now that you are five years old, you have to start taking lessons from Acharya Vishwamitra. He would teach you reading, writing, and arithmetic every morning. You will have lessons in Sanskrit and Pali languages and also be taught the Vedas and the Upanishads".

Tathagata was excited that he would be walking every day to Guru Vishwamitra's *ashram* outside the palace gate and that he would meet the children of the extended royal family. He looked forward to starting these lessons at the end of the summer season.

The day after the birthday celebrations was a sad day for him. In the morning, Yashodhara left in a horse carriage to go back to Devadaha. He had very much liked playing with her during the last couple of days and wished that the celebrations could occur more often so that she would come back to attend them. But he also knew why these celebrations did not take place more often. That is a very sad story of Tathagata's birth, which he must tell you now.

It was five years ago that he was born on a full moon day of *Vaisakha* under a *Sala* tree, which was within the premises of the Lumbini Gardens near Kapilvastu. His mother Queen Maya was traveling that day in a palanquin going to her parent's palace at Devadaha, the capital of the neighboring Koliya state. As per the customs of the day, she was going with her entourage to her parental home for the birth of her child. She stopped midway at the Lumbini Gardens to rest. As she was walking around the gardens appreciating the flowers in bloom, the labor pains started.

The attending ladies made a circle around her to help, and after a while, Tathagata was born under a *Sala* tree. Now that the queen had already given birth, there was no need to go to her parent's house and the party turned back to go back to Kapilvastu. Tathagata's father Raja Suddhodana was extremely happy to welcome the queen into Kapilvastu with the new-born prince. There were celebrations all over Kapilvastu for the birth of the first child who would be the future Raja.

On the fifth day after his birth, there was a naming ceremony held in the palace, and he was named Siddhartha, the one who succeeded in his mission. His mother Queen Maya was very happy that she had a son in her lap to offer to Raja Suddhodana as his descendant. Tathagata's parents had waited for a long time for this to happen, and now they were overjoyed to see his face. Tathagata was told that he was a big baby, tall and fair with the sharp features of his beautiful mother. The palace priest and astrologer Asita had come to deliver the *Jataka*, the birth chart, and predicted that he had the potential to be a great king - a *Chakravarty*. Asita also said that there was as much possibility that he could be a great religious leader – a *Mahapurusha*.

Tathagata's mother Queen Maya had not yet fully recovered from the rigors of the child-birth. She was high in her spirit, but physically very frail and ailing. The king had assembled a team of the best *Ayurveda* and other medical experts and assistants to cure the ailing queen. But suddenly, on the seventh day after Tathagata's birth, his mother's condition deteriorated. Although there were the best efforts and wishes of the whole kingdom of Kapilvastu, his mother Queen Maya breathed her last that day in the evening. His father was shattered due to these turns of events and did not come out of the bedroom for a few days.

Tathagata was, in the meantime, looked after by the palace ladies during those terrible sad days.

On the fifth day after his mother's death, his maternal uncle and Yashodhara's father Raja Dandapani arrived in Kapilvastu along with his younger sister Princess Prajapati. They wanted to console Tathagata's father and attend to the religious rites to be performed for his mother's soul to rest in peace. His aunt Prajapati, who was about ten years younger than his mother, immediately took charge of his care. She had many of the features of his mother and was a beautiful young lady with a very kind heart, that was full of love and compassion for anyone who came in contact with her. She had dearly loved her elder sister Maya and wanted to make sure that Tathagata was given the best care offered by the world. He was the precious remembrance of her departed sister, and she gave all the love she could.

The religious rites for Tathagata's mother were completed on the tenth day of her death. There were feasts on the tenth and the eleventh days for the relatives, friends, and members of the Brahman community, and also for the poor people. His uncle Raja Dandapani left the following day to go back to Devadaha, but he left behind his young sister to look after Tathagata. So, his aunt Princess Prajapati took up the complete burden of rearing him, ever since he was only two weeks old.

Two months passed this way. Tathagata was growing up rapidly. He was smiling, turning over, and recognizing the faces. His father took quite some time to recoup from the loss of his mother. For the first few weeks after the death, he rarely saw Tathagata and plunged himself more and more into the administration of the kingdom. Then he started coming more often to see Tathagata in his aunt's quarters when he was three months old. Tathagata was then already smiling and looking at his father's eyes. His father would then come and sit down to take him in his arms and would keep on gazing at his face and talking with his aunt about Tathagata, his mother, and his aunt Prajapati's family back in Devadaha. Talking with his aunt helped his father to regain balance in his life. Tathagata's welfare and the remembrance of his mother were the two common forces that united both of them together, and they started liking each other's company. Tathagata was at the center of their attention, and that brought both of them closer to each other as the days and weeks passed by. Finally, one day his father asked his aunt Prajapati, whether she would consent to be his wife and be a mother to Tathagata. His aunt was ready and gladly accepted the proposal. Both of them contacted his aunt's family in Devadaha and obtained full agreements from her family. Tathagata's father then announced at the royal court that, a simple marriage ceremony would occur between him and Princess Prajapati during the coming days. Everyone in Kapilvastu was very sympathetic, supported this proposal, and thought that this was the best that could have happened within the circumstances.

As proposed, a simple marriage ceremony was held within a week at the palace temple, and the Brahman priests, performing the marriage rites in front of the fire, blessed the couple in the presence of a small number of guests from Kapilvastu and Devadaha. The couple took the marriage vows and garlanded each other. There was no big feast, but there was only the distribution of sweets and snacks to all the guests. Thus, Tathagata's aunt Prajapati, also known as Gautami, became his second mother, and she was the real mother he grew up with, never missing the love of the mother, who gave him birth. Since Gautama was their family title, indicating a genesis from Rishi Gautama, Tathagata also became known as Siddhartha Gautama.

With Queen Gautami as his wife, Tathagata's father started a new chapter in his life. She took complete charge of making all the arrangements for Tathagata's care and feeding. A few wet nurses were employed to feed him. There were attendants to bathe and clean him. The Raja and the Queen would take him around the gardens in the evening. Soon he started crawling and then taking steps on his own. He would crawl all over the rooms downstairs in the palace. He started talking when he was barely a year old and called Queen Gautami *Matasri* and called his father *Pitasri* in his babbling tongue. Years passed by, and he had a very quiet, normal, peaceful, and protected childhood within the four walls of the palace.

Both of Tathagata's parents were always concerned about the predictions of the astrologer Asita, that Tathagata might become an ascetic rather than a great king. So, they made sure that he was never exposed to the horrors and tragedies of life. They also kept him away from the public glare at that time, when he was still a baby. For that reason, they would not celebrate his birthdays in a big public manner, as they did when he was five years old. Normally, they would just have a simple birthday puja for him at the palace temple. His parents would give him new clothes, toys, and gifts before the puja in the morning. This year, they decided to hold the birthday celebrations in a big way, because Tathagata had become five years old, and time had healed the wounds around the sad events relating to his mother Queen Maya's death.

●●●

Tathagata and Yashodhara at the Birthday Party

-2-

Student days

At the end of the summer, Tathagata started going to Guru Vishwamitra's *ashram* school outside the palace gate. The school had about forty students who participated in the learning programs, and all of them belonged to the ruling *Kshatriya* caste of Kapilvastu. They included the sons of the extended royal family and the court nobles. The lessons were specifically targeted at the children of the warrior caste. A student attended the school for ten years to complete the program. They were divided into two groups of students: the junior group with less than five years of attendance, and the senior group with five to nine years of attendance. Tathagata joined the junior group, where there were about twenty students. There were four new students, who started with the junior group, and he was one of the four. His cousin Aniruddha, who was his paternal uncle's son, also started school with him. His paternal cousin Devadatta was another new student in his group.

The classes started early in the morning and continued for about four hours. The students were taught chanting, reading, writing, and arithmetic in the morning. They were sent home an hour before noon for lunch and rest. The classes in the afternoon lasted for two to three hours and generally focused on detailed discussions about religious scriptures, social customs, and the laws of the land.

On the first day of school, Tathagata's father took him to Guru Vishwamitra's *ashram* to talk to the guru about the specific study plans and then dropped him off. Tathagata had brought with him a newly purchased writing slate and sticks of writing chalks for the slate. Guru Vishwamitra gave individual attention to each student while giving the group instructions.

They were first taught the alphabet. The guru wrote on the slate all of the first twelve alphabets corresponding to the 'short' and 'long' vowel sounds, for example, a, ā, i, î, u, ū, e, ē, o, ō, r, ř, etc. During the following days, the guru taught him the alphabet for three dozen consonant sounds. He was very excited to learn the four dozen alphabets, both the vowels and the consonants during the first week itself. Guru Vishwamitra said, "Siddhartha, you have done well to learn all the alphabet in the first week. I will show you next how to compose different words."

Tathagata was shown how to combine consonants and vowels by writing equivalent vowel notations (and not the separate alphabets) before, after, on top, or bottom of the consonant alphabet. He was excited to learn this quickly and was able to write many words using this technique. Please see Appendix E where the Devanagari vowel and consonant scripts used today are shown since they closely resemble what was used then.

After two weeks of the above exercises, Tathagata was shown a list of the complex consonants – the additions of two consonant sounds and how to write them. This was a list of about eighty commonly used complex consonant characters and their writing styles. This took him another two weeks to master. So, at the end of the first month, he had completely practiced the complex consonant characters and the associated writing styles. Please see Appendix F, where these complex consonant characters in Devanagari script are listed.

The descriptions in the above Appendices should give you an idea about the vowels, consonants, and complex consonant characters that Tathagata worked with. It was fortunate that his forefathers had already scientifically designed a complete set of alphabets based upon phonetic science, and one could write any desired sound unambiguously.

The next challenge was to write full sentences and small paragraphs. These exercises continued for months, with the complexity of the compositions increasing step by step. As part of the composition exercises, Tathagata was also taught the rules of grammar, especially for the Sanskrit language. Sanskrit could be similarly written in the script of any of the Indian languages. It should be noted that there was a taboo at that time against writing of sacred religious texts and one was expected to memorize such material.

The second part of the morning sessions was devoted to teaching arithmetic. Tathagata was taught the reading and the writing of the numbers up to one hundred in the first week. They were then asked to write and remember the multiplication tables up to ten times ten. This took another week to master. The next challenge was to learn and remember the multiplication tables up to 25 times 10. They achieved that in a month. Now Tathagata was given the simple arithmetic problems to solve. As he advanced, he was given more and more complex arithmetic problems to solve.

During the afternoon sessions, they focused on the learning of the sacred scriptures, such as the Vedas and the Upanishads. They chanted all of the Vedas (Rig, Sama, Yajur, and Atharva), as instructed and chanted by Guru Vishwamitra. The guru then explained the meaning and the purpose of these hymns. Understanding and mastering these scriptures took years of continuous practice and coaching.

Tathagata's mother Queen Prajapati was very concerned that he was spending all of his time, doing only studying and school work. His father concurred with that observation. So, they organized games in the mornings and the afternoons during the school holidays. It was compulsory that Tathagata participated and led in these activities. Musical events were also held in the evenings during all the school holidays, and he took part in them regularly. During the following long summer holidays, he had lessons on playing the flute. After learning that, he played the flute, whenever he got a chance during the musical events.

Tathagata especially remembers one incident during the student days. It was during the festival holiday and he had accompanied his parents to an agricultural ceremony. His father was marking off the start of the cultivation season and was tilling a piece of the land with a plow, which was heavily decorated. Tathagata was left to rest under the shade of a rose apple tree nearby. After waiting there for some time, he got into a meditative mood and sat cross-legged under the rose apple tree. After a little while, he got into a trance. That was his first direct experience of the precious feeling of sublime happiness. He was unaware of his separate existence and was one with the universe. When his parents returned, they were surprised to see him in a deep meditative trance. They were reminded of the predictions of the priest Asita and Kaundinya at the time of his birth.

The years passed by very fast, and soon Tathagata was ten years old and completed junior years at the *ashram*. He was ahead of all the students in his group, and his parents were very happy that he was very active and enthusiastic in all of the activities.

Now that Tathagata was ten years old and part of the senior group at the *ashram*, he had to only attend the morning classes. These classes were devoted to advanced discussions of the literature and the scriptures in the first half of the morning session. They then had discussions on history, politics, and law. There were no afternoon classes in the *ashram* for the senior group. But they had to attend the classes at the *Akhada*, where they got training and practice on horse riding, archery, swordsmanship, wrestling, bodybuilding, and battle formations. His favorite sports were horse riding, archery, and battle strategies. He loved to ride on his horse Kanthaka and compete with the other riders. He was also excellent in archery and could shoot the targets consistently. As he acquired more battle ground techniques, he considered strategies where there would be minimal loss of men and materials during the battles.

The *Akhada* house was also used in the evenings as the entertainment center for the young people and they played the games of chess, squares, and *Ludo*.

As Tathagata was completing his education and training, certain things that bothered him. One of the things was the fact that knowledge was being restricted to only a few advantaged persons, and the whole society was being kept in ignorance. Persons of lower castes were not being encouraged to learn the scriptures. They were even not allowed to chant the sacred hymns in many of the instances. The Brahman priests and scholars closely guarded the scriptures and did not teach them to members of low caste. Most of the scriptures were being composed in the scholarly Sanskrit language and not in the locally spoken languages of the people. This made it difficult for the common people to understand the religious discourses. Tathagata was not for these kinds of restrictive customs of the society. He wanted to do something one day to remove these injustices in society.

●●●

-3-

The Swan Story

It was a spring morning. Tathagata was taking a stroll in the garden behind the palace. The marigolds, the champaks, the hennas, and the jasmines were in full bloom at the time. The mango and jack fruit trees and the leeches were heavily laden with the fruits. The mynas and the woodpeckers were chirping merrily. Tathagata was in a very happy mood because he had just completed both the five-year program of morning studies with guru Vishwamitra and the afternoon training in the *Akhada* on body-building and battle strategies. Henceforth he was free to help his father Raja Suddhodana in the administration of Kapilvastu.

It had been a long journey completing the ten years of studies with Guru Vishwamitra and the five years of training at the *Akhada*. Tathagata would be fifteen in a few months on *Vaisakha Poornima*, the full moon day of the summer. He would be free to spend his time as he liked, except that he would be attending the durbar held by his father for a couple of hours in the mornings.

Tathagata sat down on a bench at a quiet corner of the garden. Suddenly, there was a loud fluttering sound, and he saw a wounded swan falling upon the ground in front of him. He rushed to pick up the swan and then took it inside to bandage its wounds. The swan seemed to be in a stable state after he gave it a little water to drink and some grains to eat.

A few moments later, Tathagata saw his cousin Devadatta rushing inside the garden. Devadatta saw that Tathagata was holding the swan in the lap and caressing it gently. Devadatta said, "Siddhartha, give me that swan, I shot it down with my arrows. So, it belongs to me."

Tathagata said, "Devadatta, the bird fell wounded in front of me. I have just nursed it back to a stable state. It needs further care. Since I nursed it back to life from the edge of death, I should keep it."

Devadatta said, "Siddhartha, you should know as a *Kshatriya* that the hunter who aims the arrow accurately on the target gets the prey for him to keep and use as he wants. You are going against the rules set down by the elders!"

They went to Guru Vishwamitra to resolve the dispute. Who owns the wounded swan, Devadatta who successfully shot it down, or Siddhartha who saved its life? Guru Vishwamitra said, "The swan belongs to neither of you. Siddhartha should release it, once it recovers from its wounds and regains its flying capacity."

Tathagata was allowed to keep the bird to nurse it and then release it in a few days. He was very happy to receive this verdict from Guru Vishwamitra. He procured a large birdcage and put the swan inside so that it did not escape before it fully recovered. Every day he would first feed the swan at breakfast, lunch, and dinner times before he accepted his meals. He would clean up the cage himself and apply the ointments to its wounds. It was almost two weeks before the swan fully recovered, and then he brought out the swan in the cage to the palace garden and opened the door of the cage. It had to be coaxed to get out of the entrance gate of the cage. It took a few steps on the ground and then flew away. Tathagata was very happy to see it fly into the far blue sky and be free.

Tathagata was happy that he was able to save the bird from the clutches of Devadatta and thus could save its life. Otherwise, it would have been good material for a sumptuous meal prepared in Devadatta's kitchen.

This incident brought out in Tathagata a further awareness of the need to treat all the living creatures of the world in a non-violent manner, and that violence of any kind should be avoided, especially the killing of an animal or bird, where it was not warranted. He was against the hunting of wild animals, such as tigers, lions, bears, and elephants for fun and as royal sports. These wild animals had as much right as human beings to live and share the resources of the world in their respective spheres. Of course, Tathagata realized at the time that human beings often hunt animals, such as deer, rabbits, birds, etc. for food, as and when necessary for their survival. There is nothing wrong if one eats non-vegetarian food as part of maintaining life. But it must be done thoughtfully by giving proper weight to the sanctity and preservation of life. For example, it would not be a good thing to kill baby animals before they would have a chance to experience more of life.

Tathagata had realized then that the customs of sacrificing the animals and the birds at alters during the religious ceremonies were especially very unjust and cruel. These violent rituals and sacrifices to please the heavenly gods were undoubtedly wrong and very unwarranted.

●●●

- 4 -

Tathagata's World

Tathagata was now almost fifteen years old and ready to learn the ropes of administration from his father. It was appropriate for Tathagata to talk about the Shakya country and the surrounding republics and kingdoms so that one could better appreciate the customs, rituals, and political forces governing the society at those times.

Tathagata's father Suddhodana was the Raja of the Shakya *Janapada* or republic. The country was ruled by a council called Shakya *Parishad* with members from the warrior and other castes engaged in running the administration. The *Gana Pramukh* or Raja was elected by the council and served for life unless removed by the council for some reason. The Raja generally came from select warrior families and was the male head of a particular household. Important decisions were always taken after deliberations in the council and by overall agreement by the members and very seldom by numerical voting. The Raja had considerable power to administer the country effectively.

The *Sansthagara* or the administration building of the Shakya republic was in the center of Kapilvastu. Deliberations on important questions were held there and anyone above the age of fifteen could attend these meetings, although only the members of the council were allowed to speak. One could become a member of the council only after attaining the age of twenty. Raja Suddhodana chaired such meetings.

Raja Sihahanu, the father of Raja Suddhodana, was a descendant of the legendary King Ikshvaku. Raja Sihahanu had married Kaccana, a Koliya princess from Devadaha and they had five sons and two daughters. Raja Suddhodana was one of the five sons. As earlier mentioned, he had married Princess Maya and later Princess Prajapati. They were the two daughters of Anjana, the Koliya princess and the sister of Kaccana. Queen Amita was the sister of Raja Suddhodana and was married to Raja Dandapani, brother of Princess Prajapati. Thus, the two families had marital relations between them for generations. It was a common practice to marry maternal cousins from the other clan.

The Koliya Republic was on the eastern side of river Rohini and Devadaha was its capital. Both of these republics were annexed by the kingdom of Kosala and hence they operated as vassal states. Shravasti was the capital of Kosala.

Further east of Koliya Republic was the Malla Republic and Kusinara was its capital. Malla also was a vassal state under the kingdom of Kosala.

Southeast of Malla republic was Lichchavis republic and Vaishali was its capital. Eight of the clans including Lichchavis, Videhans, Jnatrikans, and Vrije's had formed a confederacy of republics with Vaishali as its capital. It stretched from river Gandaki on the west touching the Malla Republic to river Koshi on the east and covered the area below the Himalayas north of the river Ganga. This confederacy was called Vrije Maha *Janapada* or Vrije

Federation and was one of the largest such confederacies. Each of these eight republics was autonomous and independent. The confederacy primarily managed issues relating to external security. There were representatives from every district of the confederacy and they met in Vaishali as the situations demanded.

South of the river Ganga was the kingdom of Magadha. Its capital was Rajagriha, which was very strategically located, surrounded by five hills and stone fortifications.

Vatsa was a kingdom north of Magadha on the south side of the river Ganga and Kaushambi was its capital. Kaushambi was located on the river Yamuna, not too far from its confluence with the river Ganga at Prayag.

The kingdom of Avanti was situated west of Vatsa and was an important trading state because river Narmada connected it to the southern and the western territories and the sea.

Rivers Ganga, Yamuna, and Narmada were the main arteries for trade between all of these states at the time. There was a trading route from Rajagriha on the south to Shravasti on the north and from there westward to Takshasila in Gandhara. Kaushambi was also connected to Shravasti and Rajagriha.

Tathagata would now give a picture of the social and economic environment at that time. Agricultural societies had been already established on a wide scale in the villages and they had much success. Hence, towns and cities had sprung up to provide support for farming and trading activities and acted as the administrative control centers of the republics and the kingdoms. The caste system had been established in the villages to provide different services to the farming communities. The businessmen and the traders in the towns were relatively more prosperous by providing products and services to the surrounding village communities and by carrying out commerce between the cities and the states.

The four Vedas (Rig, Sam, Yajur, and Atharva) had been already composed hundreds of years back and the Brahminic customs and traditions had been in place in most of the Gangetic valley. Few of the Upanishads conjecturing on the nature of the reality and other philosophical matters had been composed by then. *Rishi* Kapila had just proposed the *Sankhya* philosophy explaining the forces running behind all the phenomena in the universe. As per sage Kapila, every phenomenon including any evolution is a play between *Prakriti*, the inert matter, and *Purusha*, the universal conscious energy. There was no creation out of nothing by a creator God. Kapilvastu was said to be a city built by the students of the famed philosopher and was named in his honor.

The prosperity brought by the agrarian production of excess food created a set of people in the towns and cities who had the time to ponder over the larger questions of life. The *Shramana* movement had already started around that time. Young and old persons from different walks of life left their homes, cut off the family and marital relations, and wandered as ascetics in search of answers to the problems of the world. They sustained themselves by collecting alms of food items from the householders, at least once in the morning in the surrounding villages and towns. The residents generally took it upon themselves to help these seekers and to earn heavenly merits in the process. Some of the *Shramanas* also lived in the forests and met their needs by gathering fruits, leaves, and other foods from the forest. Free from the responsibility of earning a livelihood and running a household, the *Shramana* devoted most of his time to seeking the path of *Moksha* or ultimate deliverance.

Tathagata was excited that he had completed his studies and was ready to mingle with the world. Of course, he also needed some fun and time off, just as any young man would after years of training and hard work!

•••

-5 -

Yashodhara's Visit

Tathagata was to be fifteen years old the following day. His parents had decided to celebrate his coming of age and the completion of his studies and training. They had invited their close relatives from Devadaha to attend the celebrations. Yashodhara along with her mother Queen Pamita arrived at Kapilvastu a day before *Vaisakha Poornima*. It was ten years since they had last visited during his earlier birthday celebrations. Yashodhara was also almost fifteen years old now and had grown up to be a charming young lady. She was tall, slender, and beautiful. Her captivating eyes danced with a short smile on her face. Tathagata was struck to see Yashodhara's beauty and grace as she alighted from the chariot. Queen Gautami and Queen Pamita walked ahead. Behind them, Yashodhara and Tathagata followed while exchanging notes regarding the events that had transpired since they saw each other last.

Yashodhara said, "Siddhartha, you have grown so tall and handsome! What have you been doing? You never came to visit us at Devadaha! Why?"

Tathagata said, "You are a tall charming lady now, Yashodhara! Yes, I should have visited you all these years.

Perhaps there were no celebrative occasions! But now, I will surely visit you when you get married".

Yashodhara blushed at this comment and said, "Can you not visit us without an occasion?"

Tathagata said, "Yashodhara, I will create an occasion to visit you in the future. Be assured of that!"

Queen Pamita and Yashodhara rested for a little while to recover from their long journey since the early morning. After a couple of hours, they met for the late afternoon tea on the palace veranda.

Queen Pamita commented, "Siddhartha, you have grown to be a tall and strong young man. Now that you have finished your studies, aren't you ready for a young lady?"

Tathagata blushed and smiled. Didn't say a word! So, Queen Pamita looked at his mother and said, "Gautami, you need a daughter-in-law who would take care of you and Siddhartha. See how hard you are working!" Tathagata's mother put off these discussions saying that she would be thinking about that after the celebrations.

Tathagata took Yashodhara to his room. She sat down near the window. They could see the mighty Himalayas shining in the setting sun. Tathagata played on his flute a tune that he had learned recently. Yashodhara listened intently. After the conclusion of the tune, she said, "Siddhartha, you play the tune so nicely from the bottom of your heart! It is such a beautiful tune and is in harmony with the serenity of nature around here!"

Tathagata told Yashodhara about the lessons that he had been taking at the *Akhada* for the last five years and that he had become an excellent horse rider, and he could give her a ride on his horse Kanthaka the next day in the afternoon.

Their discussions then turned to the things that they had learned about the Vedas, the Upanishads, and the religious customs of the times. Yashodhara said, "I did not have the opportunity to go to an *ashram* school for my lessons as you did. But my parents had arranged for an *Acharya* to come to our palace and give me lessons on reading, writing, and arithmetic. My mother taught me about making different decorations, cooking special dishes, and performing the puja in front of the gods. I can also sing and chant hymns in the temple."

Tathagata was quite impressed and thought that Yashodhara had acquired enough of the skills needed to be a true princess. He said, "Yashodhara, you are an angel! I would like to play the flute and accompany you when you sing."

They had an early dinner that day in the palace banquet hall. Tathagata's father was very happy to see his sister Queen Pamita and niece Yashodhara. He asked about the health of Raja Dandapani and the events at Devadaha. Looking at Yashodhara, he commented, "You are a beautiful and gracious young lady now. How fast time moves! We have to soon find a groom for you!" Yashodhara blushed at these comments from her maternal uncle and didn't say anything.

Early on the next morning, Tathagata went to the palace temple along with Queen Pamita, Yashodhara, and his parents. He sat on the altar in front of the gods. The officiating Brahman welcomed the gods with hymns in Sanskrit and then blessed him. Queen Pamita and his parents also blessed him, one by one. There were sounds of conch and cymbals. Sweets and fruits, offered to the gods for the occasion, were distributed to everyone present. The ceremony was soon over and they came back to the palace.

For this occasion of Tathagata's fifteenth birth anniversary, a sumptuous meal had been arranged for the whole extended royal family. All of them sat down in the palace banquet hall for lunch. There was Uncle Amitodhana, the younger brother of Tathagata's father, and his family, including his sons Ananda, Aniruddha, and Mahanama.

After lunch, Tathagata took Yashodhara in his chariot to show her around the city of Kapilvastu. They drove around the city and then went up to the bank of river Rohini. At the bank of the river, both of them got down from the chariot and sat down under a Pipal tree. He played the flute, while Yashodhara listened with rapt attention. She said, "Siddhartha, you play the flute with so deep emotions, I love hearing you play the flute."

Tathagata thanked Yashodhara for her compliments and requested her to sing. Yashodhara chanted a beautiful hymn from the Vedas, while he tried to accompany her on the flute. It was a magical atmosphere, with the sun setting in the distance and shining on the flowing water of river Rohini, and all the birds chirping while on the way back to their nests. They were both quiet, just enjoying the scenery. Finally, the charioteer broke their silence and reminded them of the impending darkness. They got back on the chariot and went home straight. Queen Pamita and his mother were waiting for them.

Yashodhara and her mother stayed for another five days and every evening they would go to the river bank to enjoy the solitude of each other's company. On the last evening, they sat down at the river bank for a very long time. They both realized that it would be their last evening for a while. They kept on looking at each other's eyes. They were perhaps saying everything that they wanted to say, but did not!

Yashodhara and her mother started early the next morning for Devadaha. When she finally said goodbye, there were tears in Yashodhara's eyes. Tathagata too had felt strong emotions at the time of her parting but had it under control. He told Yashodhara that he would visit her soon!

As the hours passed Tathagata felt an air of melancholy for the loss of Yashodhara's company. This was a new and strange emotion for him. As he brooded over his conditions, it became clear to him that, for the first time in his life, he had developed a very strong attraction towards someone. He had fallen in love with Yashodhara!

During the following days, Tathagata often visited the Rohini riverside in the evening with a wish to recreate the memory of Yashodhara. As he gazed towards Devadaha sitting on the riverside, emotions deepened further and he was able to crystallize a poem in his heart. He played his flute tuning to the song and was overjoyed with the sweet emotions of love. His song came straight from the bottom of the heart, tinged with emotions of love and longing:

> Gazing far at the Eastern sky,
> Where melts the mighty Himalayas,
> The soft sun rays brilliantly shining,
> To that far side of river Rohini,
> Devadaha is calling me.

> Come to my lap, come fast,
> Bring the spring with you,
> Here is your love Yashodhara,
> Waiting eagerly for you,
> With smiling dreamy eyes.

Kapilvastu on this side,
Pulling me tight and strong,
From the new dreams,
Colorful and entangling,
In the core of my heart!

The soft evening wind,
And the gargling water in Rohini,
Raise the spirits very high,
To fly free as a love bird,
Towards that distant sky.

Where Gopa is waiting for me,
Sitting on the terrace garden,
Gazing westward at the sky,
Virtually we meet here,
At the shore of river Rohini.

There is magic in her eyes,
So beautiful and dancing with joy,
Her words, very sweet and soothing,
And the smile inviting,
I do miss my darling!

Two separate dreams,
Two different worlds,
Come together as streams,
Merge in the river Rohini,
And become one and all!

Our song of love and compassion,
Reverberates in the valleys,

It is the spring of life,
When we all get renewed with love,
At the shore of river Rohini!

Yes, at the shore of river Rohini, Tathagata had this magical feeling. This was a new experience of love and creative emotions that he had never felt before.

Tathagata stopped playing the flute as darkness fell. He walked towards Channa to take the chariot back home.

●●●

Tathagata and Yashodhara at River Rohini

-6-

Yashodhara's *Swayamvara*

Almost a year passed since Tathagata saw Yashodhara. He missed her and embellished her remembrance, but never came down to planning a trip to Devadaha to visit her. In the meantime, his parents had been talking about getting a life partner for him, so that he could get to know the pleasures and the challenges of life. That is when a messenger from Devadaha came to invite them to attend Yashodhara's *Swayamvara* ceremony to be held on the day of *Vaisakha Poornima*. He also brought a special invitation for Tathagata to compete in her *Swayamvara* and seek her hand! What a heavenly opportunity! Yashodhara had a mesmerizing spell on Tathagata during her last visit to Kapilvastu. When she left for Devadaha after a week's stay, he felt her absence for days and months. He realized for the first time in his life, how deeply he yearned for Yashodhara's company. Yes, there was no doubt he had fallen in love with Yashodhara! So, it was not difficult at all for his parents to make him agree to compete in Yashodhara's *Swayamvara* competition.

Tathagata's mother Queen Gautami was very enthusiastic about the possibility of this matrimonial tie-up. After all, Yashodhara was her brother's daughter and also the daughter of her husband's sister. So, she was more like a daughter to both of his parents. Besides, Yashodhara was such a lovely and well-behaved girl, they thought. His mother liked her immensely and wished she could be her daughter-in-law. His parents thought that Yashodhara was an excellent fit for him since she was very bright, and yet very sensitive just like him. It was a match made in the heavens!

The crux of the matter now was how to compete in the *Swayamvara* and beat all the contestants. As per Raja Dandapani, Yashodhara's father, a candidate for Yashodhara must win in the competition. Then, it was up to Yashodhara to accept the winner as her husband. Of course, there was no doubt in Tathagata's mind that if he were to win the competition, she would be the happiest person to garland him as her husband. She had become very close to him during the last summer's trip to Kapilvastu.

In the special invitation addressed to him, there was also a personal note from Yashodhara which said, "My dear Siddhartha, I wish the heavens to urge you to compete and win me over! – Your ever Yashodhara."

These words spoke volumes about the deep emotions Yashodhara felt. After she had gone back to Devadaha, it seemed, she had also missed his company. Like him, she was also in love! But, neither of them had openly avowed their love for each other. Now, Yashodhara was brave enough to express it openly and challenged him to draw closer. He felt a tremendous urge within him to put his life in line to win her over.

How about the day of *Vaisakha Poornima*, the full moon day of summer? Wasn't that his lucky birthday too? It was only providential that Yashodhara's *Swayamvara* and marriage would also take place on the same day!

Tathagata opened the special invitation and read that the contestants had to win a shooting game of archery and then participate in a race of horse riding. He was so elated to discover that. After all, these were two of his favorite sports! But he had to make sure that he could win, no matter what.

Vaisakha Poornima was only three weeks away. So, Tathagata immediately finalized his strategy to get ready for the competitive event. He wanted to practice archery every day in the afternoon at the *Akhada*. He planned every morning to practice racing with his horse Kanthaka and took expert advice to get Kanthaka ready for the race. He had to employ the right techniques to ride on Kanthaka. In the meantime, they had to keep themselves mentally and physically strong. He practiced Yogic exercises in the *Akhada* to further tone up his body and mind. Channa was instructed to serve Kanthaka the best nutritious food and ensure that his quarters were clean and free of insects.

The day before *Vaisakha Poornima*, Tathagata sent Kanthaka to Devadaha with Channa, so that Kanthaka was rested before the race. They all started the procession to Devadaha early morning on the full moon day. He was all dressed up in a silk dhoti, an embroidered jacket, and a headgear studded with shining and colorful stones. They rode in two elephants which were heavily decorated for the occasion. He rode on the first elephant leading the way. His parents rode on the second elephant following him. There was a retinue of horsemen advancing with them, giving them cover. A four-horse carriage was following them with some of the palace staff and the gifts to be given for the occasion.

After six hours of ride, their procession reached Raja Dandapani's palace at Devadaha. Tathagata was received by Yashodhara's parents and seated in the center of the decorated assembly hall on the side, where all the invited contestants waited. His parents sat down on the opposite side, where the guests were seated. There were kings, queens, princes, and princesses from the neighboring kingdoms.

Tathagata eagerly looked forward to the planned events in the late afternoon. As the eldest son and the crown prince, he was expected to wed and commence the life of a householder very soon. So, he was excited to realize that Yashodhara would be a perfect life partner for him and that she was ready and willing to garland him as her life partner. But, before Yashodhara garlanded him, he had to be declared the winner of the competition amongst the aspiring princes. Could he be the champion? That question made him nervous. When he saw Yashodhara, he had a broad smile and said, "It is your day, Yashodhara. Wish me good luck!"

Yashodhara quipped, "Oh, Siddhartha, this is your day too! Your birthday! You would surely win since I have prayed for you to win. Concentrate your meditative mind on the winning, my dear. Good luck!"

The competition started late in the afternoon. The first to be held was the archery race, shooting at the target ten times with the arrows. Tathagata was the first one to shoot, and he hit the center mark in each of the ten chances that he was allowed. So, he got a perfect score! Looking at his results, all the succeeding contestants were very nervous, and no one among them got a perfect score. This news spread rapidly throughout the celebration grounds. Yashodhara was jubilant. Tathagata's spirits were sky-high. The battle was almost won already! Now, it all hinged upon the race of horse-riding, and in the worst case, someone may win the race and equalize with him! Then, it would be for Yashodhara to decide between the two equals. He did not want the matters to go that far and wanted a clean and convincing win. He was extremely confident of himself and Kanthaka. The win in archery had given him that extra energy to make it happen. For the other competing princes, the battle was already half lost. But the horse-riding race was the only chance they had to equalize with him at best. A number of them dropped out of the race. But there were some other brave princes, who lined up for the race. It was so exciting to see the decorated horses with their masters on the saddle, dashing for the finish line. Finally, Kanthaka delivered Tathagata the victory that he wanted, and he was declared the winner of the horse-riding race too.

Tathagata's clean sweep of the *Swayamvara* competition was very sweet for him, his parents, and the entire party from Kapilvastu. Yashodhara was overtaken with joy and relieved that she had got the man of her choice. She had the man of her secret dreams, and also a man, who proved his skills in front of her parents and the world of Devadaha!

Yashodhara, along with her parents, walked towards Tathagata and his parents. She put the flower garland on Tathagata and chose him as her husband. He embraced her and kissed her with tears of joy in his eyes. He paid respects to her parents. Yashodhara paid respects to his parents. The parents of both sides embraced each other rejoicing at this new relationship.

It was now time for the formal marriage ceremony in front of the sacred fire. Tathagata first sat at the altar with his parents. The Brahman priest, chanting the slokas in Sanskrit, sanctified him first, in preparation for the marriage. Similarly, Yashodhara sat at the altar with her parents, and the Brahman priest sanctified her to prepare for the marriage. Then Yashodhara and Tathagata sat together at the altar, flanked on each side by their respective parents. The guests were seated in front of the altar in rows. Chanting the hymns in Sanskrit, while pouring ghee on the sacred fire to keep it vigorous, the Brahman priests tied the knots between the ends of his dhoti and Yashodhara's sari, to symbolize the union of their hearts and souls. Tied in this fashion, they walked around the sacred fire seven times, while the hymns solemnizing them as husband and wife were being chanted.

The marriage rites were over. Accompanied by Yashodhara, Tathagata went around to accept the blessings from their parents and elders present there.

A dinner reception had been planned for the evening. Raja Dandapani's palace was lighted, and there were sounds of music and entertainment all around Devadaha. Yashodhara and Tathagata sat on the dais of the reception hall, to interact with and accept the gifts from the guests and the well-wishers.

Tathagata still remembers that night, when Yashodhara walked into the honeymoon room, decorated with the garlands and the bouquets of the flowers and the fruits. At the center of the room, there was the decorated bed, almost covered by garlands of jasmine, champak, and henna. On the floor in front of the bed, there was a huge brass pot, where the lotus flowers were floating in the water. There was a burning candle in a floating brass jar in the middle of the pot, radiating its light on the lotus flowers. The floor around this mini pond of lotus flowers was decorated with a *Mandala*. There was a tall brass jar with a coconut on the top and the mango leaves underneath, that symbolized the fullness and the sanctity of life.

Yashodhara was wearing the light red bridal sari, studded with shining small stars of gold. She had made a veil with the ends of the sari, almost covering her face. Her feet and hands were completely decorated with red and orange color flower markings. She was wearing anklets made of gold on her feet. As Tathagata was waiting on the bed for her to come, the door opened and she was gently pushed into the room by her friends in the palace. As the door closed, Tathagata rushed to welcome her. He took out the veil from her face, embraced and held her closely under his grip, and then looked at her face, eyeballs to eyeballs. This was the first time they were ever alone this close. There was joy and longing in her eyes. They kissed each other all over and stood there embraced together. He quickly bolted the door from inside with one hand and then led her to the edge of the bed, where they sat down facing the mini lotus pond, with its floating candle shining on their faces. Yashodhara folded her hands at the sacred light, thanking the gods for fulfilling her wishes. He clasped her hands and together they thanked the forces of the world, the *Pancha Bhutas* (Five Elements), for bringing them together.

Their minds and souls were already united. Only their bodies remained to be united. They were two children, pure and unspoiled by the world as yet, and for the first time in life, they were trying to discover their bodies together. He undressed Yashodhara and kissed her all over her body. A shivering current exploded through her body and mind. She embraced Tathagata with a primordial force, that clasped them together as one united body. The full moon, shining through the window, was the witness to this union of their body and soul!

They slept deep and long in each other's embrace. The rays of the morning sun, shining through the window, woke him up. They had to prepare themselves to leave the world of Devadaha and start the procession to Kapilvastu before it was too late in the day. For the first time, he could completely see in daylight Yashodhara's beautiful body that still lay submitted to the altar of love and passion of the night before, their first night together. She looked even more beautiful than he had imagined, trying to feel her under the moonlit night. Tathagata kissed her gently on the face trying to wake her up. She opened her eyes with a half-smile on her face and kissed him back. They embraced each other for the first time in the broad daylight and looked at each other recalling the bliss of their union the night before.

Tathagata said, "Yashodhara dear, we have to get up and get ready. The world of Kapilvastu will be waiting for you tonight. We will resume our passions together in the night. For the time being, you have to get ready to leave Devadaha, for a while at least. Get up, my dear!"

Yashodhara arranged her sari and got up from the bed. She had to organize together all her things, that needed to be taken to Kapilvastu in the carriages, that would follow them. She had to say goodbye to her world for the last sixteen years. It would not be easy.

Yashodhara said, "Siddhartha dear, I will miss my parents and the people of Devadaha. I will miss our palace too! How beautiful it is to look at the Himalayas at the sunrise and the sunset from these windows! How serene and romantic it is, to lie down here and gaze at the shining moon and the hills together in the night! Promise me that you would bring me back here again and again."

Tathagata said, "Yes, dear, we would be back here. Now please get ready and instruct the servants to pack and carry your personal belongings to the carriage."

It was well past noon, by the time they got the

carriages loaded with the stuff that Yashodhara was bringing with her and the things that her parents were sending as parting gifts, for both of them, his parents and the marriage party from Kapilvastu. A caravan of dozen carriages was lined up in front of the palace. Leading the procession was the original party from Kapilvastu, the two elephants at the front, the horsemen, and the two carriages from Kapilvastu following them. Behind the caravan were the horsemen from Devadaha, guarding the whole party.

It was a tearful affair for Yashodhara to take leave from her parents, relatives, friends, and the palace staff. Queen Pamita was very emotional to bid goodbye to her only daughter. For sixteen years, Yashodhara had followed her mother as a shadow. She was her mother, teacher, and friend, all in one. It was Queen Pamita who had taught her how to behave in real life, both in good and bad situations. It was her mother, on whom Yashodhara relied for advice during her growing-up period. Queen Pamita won't be there anymore so that Yashodhara could shed tears in her arms or share the small joys of life. Queen Pamita told Yashodhara, "Gopa, I would visit you as often as I could, but Aunt Prajapati is your new mother and she would take good care of you. Uncle Suddhodana is there too as your new father. Above all, Siddhartha will be always there at your side to protect you. So, do not grieve, my dear daughter. Take good care of Siddhartha and your new parents. And always remember to keep the honor of our two families!"

With these words, Queen Pamita kissed Yashodhara on the forehead, embraced her, and then stayed back to gaze at the waiting procession. A tearful Yashodhara was the last one to come out of the palace, and Tathagata led her gently to the waiting elephant. They were both mounted on

Pahoda (canopied seats) on the leading elephant and their journey to Kapilvastu started.

It took them six hours to arrive at the outskirts of Kapilvastu. As instructed earlier by the messengers, everyone in the city knew that Tathagata was arriving in the evening with his newly wedded bride Princess Yashodhara of Devadaha. The streets of the city were decorated and lighted. A musical band party had joined the procession as they entered the city. Men, women, and children were lined up on both sides of the main street, starting from the east gate, all the way to the palace walls. They were welcomed by the slogans of 'Long live Prince Siddhartha and Princess Yashodhara.' There were also special blessings performed by the women folks at all the important street corners. Finally, they arrived inside the palace gate. Tathagata led Yashodhara to the main door of the palace. They were welcomed by both of his parents with ritual blessings and the vermillion marks on their foreheads. They were led to the newly decorated bedroom, that was to be theirs henceforth. The bedroom was decorated with flowers, bouquets of fruits, and garlands similar to what was done in Devadaha. This would be their first night together in the palace in Kapilvastu and hence, everyone wanted them to start here in the best possible romantic environment.

For sure, they were tired from the long journey from Devadaha and retired early to an evening of uninterrupted solitude in their bedroom. It was a blissful and magical night again for both of them at the palace in Kapilvastu.

The following day was a day of celebration. Yashodhara and Tathagata visited the palace temple in the morning. Customary rites were performed by the Brahman priest. They were blessed by the elders of the royal family, the relatives, and the close friends.

A big feast and reception had been planned for the evening. Musical events were held at the open stage in the palace garden. The feast was being served to thousands of citizens of Kapilvastu. They sat in the reception hall to interact with and receive gifts from the attending guests.

Tathagata's parents were very happy that Yashodhara had finally come back to Kapilvastu as their daughter-in-law. They could sense the sparks of love and rapture between Tathagata and Yashodhara. They were now certain that she would bring good luck and prosperity to their lives at Kapilvastu!

●●●

Yashodhara garlands Tathagata at her *Swayamvara*

-7-

Life in the Palace

Tathagata and Yashodhara settled down gradually to married life in the palace at Kapilvastu. A two-floor palace wing was allotted to them at the back corner of the palace. From their bedroom on the second floor, they could look at the backside of the palace garden and the wooded area of the palace grounds. The snow-capped mountains of the Himalayan range could be seen glittering over the woods on clear days. It was a beautiful environment that brought them closer to each other every day that they lived there. They spent most of their time together relaxing in each other's company, seldom venturing outside the palace.

Queen Gautami was so kind and caring to Yashodhara that she felt she was more of a daughter at Kapilvastu, and hence she missed Devadaha and her parents less and less. She had met many of the palace staff before but came to know all of them more intimately, especially the kitchen staff and the personal staff attached to their palace wing. She decorated the bedrooms and the meditation room upstairs. The drawing room and the entertainment room downstairs were refurbished and given a new lease of life. They often held music and entertainment evenings downstairs in their wing of the palace.

The palace kitchen was situated in the middle of the backside of the palace. It was a huge open courtyard, around which there were store-rooms, cutting rooms, cooking rooms, and dining halls. Yashodhara worked with the kitchen staff to ensure that some of the favorite items were prepared every day, during breakfast, lunch, and dinner. Food was usually served in the family dining hall, except on formal occasions, when they were served in the banquet hall. Sometimes, food would be served in their private palace wing and they would eat together downstairs in their wing. They would have the late-night snacks often served that way downstairs.

Life was beautiful and very enchanting during those years. So many small and big pleasures of life were available to them. Yashodhara and Tathagata deeply loved each other and could not withstand any separation between them. The years passed by quickly this way.

During one of their marriage anniversary celebrations, Tathagata's father said, "Siddhartha, I want you and Yashodhara to have new palace wings built such that you would have better and more spacious accommodations. You can build three separate wings, each one optimizing the comforts for the specific season: summer, rain, and winter. Go and consult with the state architects and builders and get them built in the coming years. These are the special gifts that we are offering to you and Yashodhara!"

Yashodhara and Tathagata worked days and nights from that day to make that a reality. As per his parents' suggestion, it was appropriate to build three separate wings, one for each season, rather than to compromise on the level of comfort provided.

After considerable analysis of the terrain around the

palace at Kapilvastu, they decided to build three separate wings at three different sites, close to the existing palace and connected through the covered corridors. The summer palace wing was a two-storied stone and brick building on the hilly top. The ground floor was used for reception and entertainment and had large halls with covered verandas around to keep them cool. The large windows installed on both the floors had specially designed shutters, that kept the sunlight curtailed during the middle of the day. The top floor rooms had curved high roofs and covered balconies all around to cool the rooms. All the rooms had marble floors to keep the rooms cool. The summer palace wing was surrounded by the trees and the woods on the three sides, to further cool the environment.

The palace wing for the rainy season was built on a leveled plot on high ground, so that water drained fast and did not accumulate or soak the ground for long, thereby increasing the humidity. This was also a two-story building with a beautiful view of the woods and the mountains. The building was surrounded by flower gardens, but with no tall trees around to make it shady and humid during the rains. This was a stone and brick building with flat roofs and with marble floors.

The winter palace wing was designed with wooden planks so that it could be more easily heated during the winter by using the burning wood in the fireplace. This was a two-storied structure built entirely with wooden studs, beams, and rafters, and also with the wooden floors covered by the area carpets in the bedrooms and the entertainment areas. The top roof was flat with a slight tapering for the water to roll down.

Each of these buildings took two years to build and furnish. Consequently, it took them almost six years to build and furnish these new palace wings. Yashodhara was intimately involved in the design, furnishing, and decoration of all these buildings, and this kept them busy for a very long time. They started using these buildings as they became available. They often held musical events in these buildings. In the rainy season, for example, they would be almost confined to staying in this palace wing for most of the time, having continuous music and entertainment downstairs. Sometimes, Tathagata would play the flute. Yashodhara would sing often, and then he would accompany her on the flute. They would also invite local talents to participate in these musical events held in the palace buildings.

Yashodhara and Tathagata had adopted a few pets during these years. They had a large number of colorful fishes in the fountain located in the garden. There were two giant turtles and a few deer and peacocks roaming around the garden. They visited the garden every morning and evening, to make sure that the pets were fed and taken care of.

As Tathagata had said earlier, he regularly attended the durbar hall meetings every morning. Tathagata was not a member of the state council of Kapilvastu and had no voting rights during the deliberations. But he had the full rights as a young Shakya prince to listen, and where appropriate, participate in the discussions.

These durbar hall meetings were very educational and often entertaining. People from all walks of life in Kapilvastu came there bringing their problems and complaints. The council was supposed to devise solutions to the problems and deliver justice in the case of civil and criminal complaints. All the solutions and judgments were debated thoroughly, taking into consideration all of the facts, figures, and witness statements. They were also supposed to satisfy the multiple groups with their divergent agenda. Tathagata's father managed these discussions deftly and stewarded the council proceedings for the overall good of the state of Kapilvastu. There were also discussions about the conflicts with the neighboring states and the issues of war and peace. During the first couple of years, Tathagata was an eager listener, never missing a day of these proceedings. As time went by, he learned enough to participate in the discussions. These discussions built the foundations of his understanding of the intricate play of the different forces in the political, social, and religious structures. Above all, he learned about the weaker sections of society and was strongly motivated to do good for these unfortunate classes of people.

Yashodhara and Tathagata often participated in small projects that were intended for the welfare of the children, women, and the poor. These opportunities to share their wealth and happiness purified their souls further. They were so happy together and life was so beautiful and enchanting. They deeply loved each other and worked as a pair of love birds never to separate.

Yashodhara sometimes remembered her family and friends in Devadaha and wanted to visit them. But she wanted to visit Devadaha along with Tathagata and that could not happen due to the busy nature of Tathagata's schedule. In any case, Yashodhara was a happy bird, very comfortable in her surroundings, and very happy to be married to Tathagata.

●●●

-8-

Trepidations on *Samsara*

Five years of marriage passed by very quickly for Tathagata and Yashodhara. Life was a dream, relaxed and beautiful. They were two young persons devoted to each other and growing up together to mature adults. Around this time, Tathagata was made a member of the state council of Kapilvastu. He could now materially participate in all of the deliberations at the durbar hall presided by his father and get more detailed exposure to the state administration. Henceforth, his mornings and some of the afternoons and evenings were devoted to attending the durbar regularly.

The state council was a powerful assembly whose membership was restricted to male members from the warrior *Kshatriya* ruling caste. All of the major decisions of the state were presented and debated, and decisions were taken unanimously or with the majority support of the council and the king. Citizens would also bring their problems to the council to receive judgments and directions. As Tathagata had told earlier, these meetings were eye-openers for him and exposed him to the problems that the citizens of Kapilvastu faced and the possible solutions for these grievances. The politics played between the king, the councilors, and the citizens were very intriguing and taught him many lessons for the future.

Tathagata would intently listen to the problems and the plans proposed in the council, and then give his opinion towards the working out of the solutions. His maturity and serenity during these council deliberations impressed the people and he was very much loved as the crown prince.

Tathagata had fond memories of some of the incidents during this period of his life. One such incident relates to the possibility of a war between King Prasenjit of Kosala and the republic of Kapilvastu. King Prasenjit planned to hold *Ashwamedha Yajna* to declare himself as the undisputed *Chakravarty* or Great Emperor. For that purpose, he had sent the horse along with a token contingent of soldiers to guard the horse, as it traveled to different countries of the region. When it came to and crossed the border of Kapilvastu, there was an uproar throughout Kapilvastu to wage a war against Kosala rather than accept the suzerainty of King Prasenjit with the new demands. Kapilvastu had been accepting the primacy of Kosala, but the new demands and the manner of sending the sacrificial horse to Kapilvastu were insulting. The council members were agitated and there were calls for a battle. Tathagata was not for this unnecessary battle of the egos between the two traditionally friendly countries, and hence he made powerful presentations in the council against the war.

"The battle would result in large-scale death and destruction and is not warranted. Kosala, as the bigger kingdom, has the advantage of manpower and resources against us. Why not make a new agreement and renegotiate the terms, rather than waging a war? We have nothing to fear! Let Kosala see the light of the day and come to the senses".

The council finally agreed with Tathagata's persuasion and sent a message to King Prasenjit to hold the negotiations. Ultimately, an agreement was reached and thus large-scale deaths and destructions were avoided. The members of the state council initially looked at the proposal as a sign of fear and cowardice, but later realized the benefits of peace and increasing prosperity. The citizens of Kapilvastu also greatly admired Tathagata after this incident. He came to realize how haste and hot tempers leading to wars cause many of the miseries in the world.

Tathagata did not have any direct contact with the people outside of the palace gate, except on ceremonial occasions when he accompanied his father and mother for the state events. He longed for direct glimpses of the life outside the palace grounds. His parents were always concerned about his venturing outside the palace and coming in contact with many of the depressing sights. His father arranged for him to take special rides on the appointed dates and through prepared routes. Tathagata's charioteer friend Channa was advised to take him around the approved route.

On his first such ride through Kapilvastu, accompanied by Channa, he saw an old man with a bent back supported by a walking stick slowly moving on the road. He was very much pained to see the plight of the old man and realized how old age made all human beings, without exceptions, suffer. Everyone would eventually go through this stage of life and lose the capability to see, hear, and move! How impermanent was everything in this world? After getting these thoughts, he asked Channa to turn around the chariot and go back to the palace.

He went straight to his private quarters and talked with Yashodhara about this event. Yashodhara consoled him, "Oh, Siddhartha, we are too far away from old age! Even our parents are still completely fit physically! Why worry about this now?"

He said, "I am not worried about just our lot, but the lot of all human beings. How is it that everything in the world is impermanent? Why must we suffer through this? Is there any way out?"

Yashodhara did not have an answer. She said, "Dearest, do not worry about things that you cannot alter, that is the fate of this world and it is determined by the gods only!"

Tathagata said, "Yashodhara, I want to find out someday the root cause of this, and then try to do something to remove the sorrow and the unhappiness!" With that, he embraced Yashodhara and was consoled by her sweet smile.

A few weeks later, Tathagata took another ride with Channa through the city. His father had earlier ordered that the designated streets be cleared of the beggars and all other suffering elements. As they drove to the far end of the route, someone with a large tummy and panting heavily emerged from a side road.

Tathagata asked Channa, "Who is this fellow? Why is he so distressed?"

Channa said, "My lord, this person is suffering from an incurable disease and cannot be helped."

Tathagata was very much pained to see the sight of this diseased person and the suffering that he was subjected to. He wondered about the unending list of pains and suffering caused by the ravages of the diseases visited by all human beings. He asked Channa to turn around and go back to the palace immediately.

Weeks passed by and Tathagata was again ready to

take a tour outside and Channa drove the carriage around their designated path. Suddenly, they saw a procession of people coming towards them. Four persons were carrying an inverted bed on their shoulders. A person was lying covered on the bed except for his face. Garlands of flowers were wrapped around the bed. People were chanting, "*Ram Nam Satya Hai*". Many in the band of followers had tears rolling down their faces. Tathagata asked Channa what the commotion was about. Channa said, "My lord, a dead person is being carried to the burning *ghat* for cremation by his relatives and friends."

Tathagata's mind was again agitated at the sight of the death procession, and he ordered Channa to get back to the palace immediately. He became very restless, thinking about the problems of old age, disease, and now death. He questioned, 'Is there a permanent solution to the suffering caused by old age, disease, and death?' There were no answers!

Months passed by. He still had no answers to his questions. One day he asked Channa to take out the carriage and visit the city outside. On the outskirts of the city, near a park, they saw a man wearing a yellow dhoti and covering his upper torso with a piece of yellow cloth. There was radiant happiness on his face, and he was walking very calmly on the side of the road. Tathagata asked Channa who the man was.

Channa said, "My lord, he is a *Shramana*, someone who has renounced the *Samsara* in the search for liberation or *Moksha*. He is free from the responsibilities of the family and lives by the kindness of people who offer him food."

Tathagata was very much impressed by the aura of happiness in the face of the *Shramana*. Beneath the outer crust of happiness and celebrations, Tathagata saw incessant streams of suffering and tragedies in the world around them. Yashodhara's sweet embraces and consolations lightened the pains that he felt inside his inner heart, but they were never able to eliminate them. As time passed by, he became more and more restless thinking about the problems of old age, disease, and death. He again questioned, 'Is there a permanent solution to the sufferings caused by old age, disease, and death?'

Yashodhara said, "Dearest, there will be always suffering due to old age, disease, and death. That is just part of life!"

Tathagata replied, "Gopa, there must be a way to eliminate the sufferings caused by old age, disease, and death. I must find it! This unending cycle of birth, old age, death, and rebirth cannot go on! One day I would like to go in search of that solution. Will you support me in that search?"

Yashodhara said, "I will do everything possible to support your aims in life."

Tathagata said, "Gopa, I may have to leave home one day, to become a *Shramana* in search of the solutions to life's suffering. Will you allow me to do that?"

Yashodhara said, "Dearest, you have to first raise a family and then be ready to take over the reins of the state from your father. When your son is ready to take over the reins, you can retire to the forest as a *Shramana*."

Tathagata interrupted, "Gopa, I do not want to take over the reins of the state. I can never take up arms to fight against any human being, either friend or foe. Hence, I should not be crowned as the king, since one of the principal duties of a king is to take up arms against the enemy when the need arises."

Yashodhara interrupted, "Would you not take up

arms in support of a good cause for the sake of *Dharma*?"

He said, "Gopa, I would not take up arms even for a good cause for the sake of *Dharma*. Instead, I would look for an amicable non-violent solution to the problem, so that no lives and properties were lost at the battlefields. Life was so short and full of misery as such! Why add to that misery in the name of a good cause? Did you know of a single case where violence had given a good solution to the problem, rather than causing more grief?"

Yashodhara replied, "But we must oppose the evil acts carried out by their perpetrators?"

Tathagata said, "Yes, we must oppose the evils, but not by violence. Where there is violence, there is always retributory counter-violence, thus an unending saga of misery plagues the people and the state. Therefore, Gopa, I would not like to be a king, since the people would expect me to do things, which I was not capable of doing!"

●●●

-9-

Birth of Rahula

Yashodhara arranged a special palace celebration on the occasion of completing their ten years of marriage. Tathagata and Yashodhara both were twenty-six years old now and they were at the prime of their lives. Tathagata was busy enough attending to the problems and the solutions discussed at the state council. On top of that, there was the unending personal quest regarding the question of old age, disease, and death. Yashodhara thought that a little celebration of life, focusing back on each other, would be a good thing to rejuvenate the spirits.

Yashodhara had invited her mother, Queen Pamita, to come to Kapilvastu. She had not visited them for a very long time, and this was a good occasion for her to come and bless them both. There was puja at the palace temple in the morning, and both Yashodhara and Tathagata sat at the altar of the temple and were blessed by all the elders. A special dinner was arranged for the whole extended royal family and the well-wishers. It was a lavish dinner accompanied by music and entertainment.

Before leaving in the morning for Devadaha, Queen Pamita asked Yashodhara, "Gopa, when am I going to see the little one? Now that you both have completed ten years of marriage, it is time you do everything to start a family!"

Yashodhara did not have an answer and just looked at her mother nodding in agreement. Her mother further added, "I have talked with Queen Gautami to arrange for you and Siddhartha to seek advice and to take the right steps in this regard. Does not Siddhartha want to start a family?"

Yashodhara said, "Maa, Siddhartha would very much like me to be a mother."

Queen Pamita added, "Well, Gopa, when I come to Kapilvastu next time, I want to see my grandchild!"

In the evening, Yashodhara told Tathagata about these conversations with her mother. Tathagata said, "Your mother is right in expecting a grandchild. We must try in earnest to make this happen soon. You would be so happy as a mother!"

Yashodhara quipped, "Won't you be happy as a father?"

Tathagata answered, "Yes, I would surely be happy to be a father. My parents too would be very happy to be grandparents! We have been married for ten years and yet, we have not had good luck. I do not know the mystery of creation. You must talk to *Matasri* and find out if there are things that need to be done to be blessed with a child!"

Yashodhara did talk to *Matasri* about this. She advised her to be regular and timely in her daily schedule and to worship every morning at the palace temple. She asked her to stay happy, eat and rest properly, and ensure that they don't spend too much time worrying about the problems of the world.

Yashodhara followed *Matasri's* advice and worshipped every morning at the palace temple. They spent as much time together in the afternoons and the evenings, learning and practicing music and song. Time passed quickly. The rains came and they entertained mostly inside the palace wing. The autumn and winter seasons were busy with many different celebrations inside and outside the palace. Then the spring came and the palace gardens were filled up with flowers. Their hopes also ran high. But there was no sign of good news from Yashodhara by the beginning of the summer. So, they decided that she perhaps needed a change of place, and both of them should visit her parent's house during their coming anniversary on *Vaisakha Poornima*. They had not visited Devadaha together to stay with Yashodhara's parents during all of these years.

Yashodhara was excited to visit her home along with Tathagata and made all the preparations for the trip. They left Kapilvastu with a small entourage. They traveled in the chariot with Channa. Their support staff and the guards followed them. They stopped on the way at Lumbini Gardens for some time and visited the place where he was born under the Sala tree.

Raja Dandapani and Queen Pamita had made special arrangements for them to stay two weeks at Devadaha. The section of the palace, where they had observed their honeymoon at the time of the marriage, was cleaned up and redecorated for their exclusive use.

Yashodhara was excited to see and talk to her old friends at Devadaha. Every afternoon, they took the rides in the chariot to different places around Devadaha. They also went up to the banks of river Rohini and could see the kingdom of Kapilvastu from the other side of the river. They went up to the high lands, as far as they could in the chariot, and could see the majestic snow-capped mountain capes of the Himalayan ranges. Many of the evenings, they had feasts in the palace, or they were invited for dinner by Yashodhara's friends and relatives.

That day of Vaisakha Poornima at Devadaha was like their honeymoon eleven years back when they became man and wife. On that day, they were both teenage children trying to discover their budding emotions. Today, they are both twenty-seven years of age, at the prime of their life, already experienced in life and love. Their deep love for each other was solid like rocks. They understood each other fully and wanted to always keep the other happy. Tathagata wanted Yashodhara to fully bloom into a woman and be a mother, and he was ready to be fully consumed by her river of love.

They had an early dinner with Yashodhara's parents and some of her close friends. Tathagata waited for her to come into the very room where they had consumed the wine of love for the first time. The room was decorated, exactly like the way it was done eleven years back. Yashodhara finally entered the room wearing her bridal dress, with a long veil on her face, just like that first day. Tathagata walked to the door, unveiled her face, held her tight, and looked at her face shining in the moonlight. Her eyes were dancing with love and desire for Tathagata. They kissed and stood holding each other tight. Tathagata led her to the edge of the bed, where they sat down in front of the floating and burning candle in the brass jar, just like the first time! Tathagata was thinking of the past eleven years of their life together. Hasn't she been the sweetest companion of his life? Tathagata asked Yashodhara, "Dearest, have you been happy these eleven years as my wife? I have been the happiest person with you by my side, and the years have moved very fast. It just seems like yesterday that we were first united here!"

Yashodhara said, "You know that I have been very happy and cherish you as my husband. I can sacrifice my life for you. If only we had a child, I would be totally happy! So, my love, embrace me tight, and let us be united in our quest."

With that thought, they lost themselves in each other's arms. The moon shining through the window was causing ripples of emotions in their body and mind. They felt united with each other and the world!

They spent two weeks of delightful time at Devadaha. It was time now to say goodbye to Yashodhara's parents and friends and then leave for Kapilvastu. Queen Pamita had tears in her eyes while bidding goodbye, and she said to Yashodhara, "Gopa, always remember my advice and take care of your and Siddhartha's health."

Queen Pamita turned towards Tathagata and said, "I am looking forward to hearing about your coronation. *Bhai* is getting old, and he needs you to take over the burden."

Tathagata smiled at her and did not say anything. Raja Dandapani also came to bid goodbye and asked to convey their greetings to Tathagata's parents. They started their journey back to Kapilvastu.

They reached Kapilvastu and settled down to regular life. Weeks passed by. It was another full moon day in late summer. They were enjoying the cool breeze of the night in their summer palace. Yashodhara came and sat down next to Tathagata and said, "Siddhartha dear, we might have struck lucky during our trip to Devadaha! I can tell you for sure in a couple of weeks, but I am already feeling it!"

Tathagata kissed her on both the cheeks and the forehead and said, "My dearest Yashodhara, I am so excited and happy for both of us. Let this fruit of our love blossom. That is my prayer."

These were the days of anxiety, excitement, and waiting. Finally, Yashodhara declared after a month that she was pregnant. She informed *Matasri* and there was jubilation in the palace. The next morning, *Matasri* accompanied Yashodhara to the temple and Yashodhara was blessed by the gods!

Yashodhara and Tathagata enjoyed every moment that they had together to feel and wait for this welcome intruder in their midst. As months passed, he could see the bulge in Yashodhara's tummy. In the evening, he would often gently feel her belly and they would both try to feel the kicks and turns of the baby inside her. Fortunately for them, Yashodhara did not have any major discomfort during the whole pregnancy period. The day of the reckoning drew closer and closer. They were getting ready and arranged for a couple of midwives and wet nurses at the palace.

The day of the arrival of the baby came. It was a full moon evening too. Perhaps the moon god had a deep connection with them! But it was a day of the eclipse, and Rahu monster almost totally ate away the moon, for quite some time! Yashodhara did labor for quite a while, but her strong will made her withstand the long labor with equanimity. Finally, their baby boy came out before midnight. The baby's intermittent cry woke up the whole palace. When Tathagata was told of the good news, he rushed to the adjoining delivery room. Yashodhara was lying on the bed, exhausted but relieved, looking admiringly at the baby sucking her breast. Her eyes met Tathagata's as he walked into the room, and there was an air of jubilation. He was very happy that finally, the ordeal was over, and they had reached their target together. They were the new parents, and their parents became the new grandparents!

Both Yashodhara and her baby were doing very well and hence they planned the naming ceremony on the fifth day. Since the boy was born on the day of the eclipse, when Rahu was out causing mischief, they named him Rahula, the one who saves the world from the clutches of Rahu!

Rahula soon found a place in their bed between Tathagata and Yashodhara and kept them busy demanding their attention. What a delight it was to look at him sucking at his mother's breast with full force, or lock his eyes with Tathagata's, trying to recognize him! It was not sufficient to just hold him close, he needed to be rocked continuously.

Rahula was a delightful child. Soon he started to turn from side to side and then sat unassisted. It was not long before he started moving around supported by his hands and knees. They had to watch him every moment to ensure his safety. Then suddenly, he was able to stand up one day, holding the edge of our bed, and then take a few steps towards Tathagata, as he called him by name. What a joy it was to see him do that! When Tathagata came home in the afternoon for lunch, Rahula would jump to his lap from his mother and play with him. He was already saying Ma-Ma to his mother and it was right after that he called Tathagata Ba-Ba, prompted by Yashodhara. Rahula was getting very attached to Tathagata and he enjoyed every moment of it!

•••

-10-

Leaving Home

Tathagata and Yashodhara observed Rahula's first birthday anniversary in a big way. His parents were very happy that their first grandchild was to be one year old. The grandson represented to them the continuity of their lineage by another generation. So, this was a major milestone for the family and must be celebrated. They had also invited Yashodhara's parents to join them in this celebration for their grandson. Yashodhara beamed with love and pride for her little hero. With all the attention that he had received, Rahula had already become a little naughty. He would run around the rooms and throw things around. Of course, everything was excused for him when he giggled at you, babbling in his baby talk!

Tathagata and Yashodhara held a big feast on the evening of Rahula's birthday. Most of Kapilvastu was there to felicitate the whole family. It was also thought that this would be the last big celebration for Tathagata's father, since Tathagata was expected to take over more of the family burden and state administration, now that he was almost twenty-nine years old. That way, he was expected to learn the ropes of both the family and the kingship, and then be ready for taking over the reign completely at a future date. Everyone in Kapilvastu was there to congratulate Yashodhara and Tathagata and their parents. There were plenty of gifts for Rahula to play and mess up with. Yashodhara's parents stayed with them for some more days, and little Rahula had a busy time, keeping his other grandparents happy.

Now Yashodhara and Tathagata had achieved one of the main aims of their marriage from the family point of view: that of bringing up a progeny to keep the continuity of life. Tathagata thought this might be a good time to prepare for a redirection of his life. The problems of old age, disease, and death, that had continuously bothered him in the background for all these years, had not gone away. These concerns resurfaced, as he was reexamining his life to plan for his eventual exit to become a *Shramana*.

The following week, Tathagata met his father one evening and said, "*Pitasri*, I have been listening all these years to the deliberations at the council. There are wide-ranging problems of poverty, sickness, and ignorance. There is also rampant corruption due to the greed, selfishness, and immorality of administrators. I note that you have to make many compromises, just for the sake of carrying everyone along. Adding to the misery is the fact that the neighboring states are always in a state of conflict with us, and they are ready to take up arms at the slightest pretext. In this environment, I do not like to take up the responsibility of kingship ever, because I cannot compromise, and I cannot lift arms against others. I would rather devote my life to the quest for the solution to the problems of suffering due to old age, disease, and death! Now that Rahula is one year old, I would like to leave home and become a *Shramana* in search of solutions. I need your blessing to be successful in this mission."

Tathagata's father was somewhat surprised at the timing of this outburst. He knew that Tathagata was inclined towards going the holy route, but he did not think, it was the right time to take the plunge. He said, "Siddhartha, you have plenty of time to search for the truth after you are fifty, just like your ancestors had done earlier. You have an infant son, who needs you. The whole kingdom is looking towards you to take over the responsibility from me after a few years. Why do you want to abandon Yashodhara, Rahula, and the family at this time? Think it over carefully."

Tathagata was persistent in his assertions and said, "*Pitasri*, I do not know how long it will take me to find the truth. I must start now when I am young so that I will have the time and perseverance for the quest. If ever I become successful in finding the truth, to eradicate the sufferings of the people, I would need further time to spread the truth all over."

His father relented somewhat and said, "Have you talked with Yashodhara and your mother about this decision? You must get Yashodhara's consent in any such plan!"

"I will talk to them soon, *Pitasri*", Tathagata said, nodding his head in agreement.

The following day, Tathagata talked to his mother queen Gautami about his plans to become a *Shramana*. His father had already told her about the conversations he had with Tathagata. She said, "Siddhartha, though my sister Maya gave you birth, I have been your real mother for twenty-nine years. I have spent all my waking hours, thinking and planning for your care, comfort, and long-term success in life. How can I now allow you to the forest, uncared for and alone in the wilderness? Maya would not have allowed such a thing either! How could my mother's heart live in peace in the palace, knowing that my son was running hungry somewhere in the forest? Though you are a father now, for me you are also that infant son, who would run to my lap at the sound of the thunder. I would miss you here every moment of my life. Your father would miss you very much, though he did not say anything like that to you. How can we console young Yashodhara and infant Rahula? Think about these things, son! Wait at least for some years till Rahula grows up. Remember, you cannot plan this unless Yashodhara consents."

Tathagata said, "*Matasri*, I owe my life to you and I would not ever do anything that would hurt your feelings. I will take leave from you all, only temporarily, and I will return for sure to share the truth that I might find one day. Bless me so that I come back and bring happiness to the world!"

She said, "I always wish you success and happiness! Talk to Yashodhara."

In the evening, Tathagata had a heart-to-heart talk with Yashodhara. His plans were not news to her, just the timing of it! Yashodhara was sympathetic and understood the turmoil inside him. She wanted him to wait some more years until Rahula grew up. Tathagata said, "I must do this while my body is still strong to withstand the rigors of the wandering life. Otherwise, I might succumb during this mission."

He further added, "Gopa, you are the only one I have ever loved. We have traveled life together long, and you have been a source of deep support and understanding for me during these years. I am asking you today to set me free, as a token of your love for me and the wider world. Only then, I can dedicate myself to the quest for solutions to the suffering of the people. You have now the burden of raising Rahula in my absence. Of course, my parents and everyone in the palace would support you. And remember, I will come back to Kapilvastu to share the truth if ever I find it."

Yashodhara said, "I have always loved you and given you my full support. I will support your latest decision too. But please allow me some more time."

Tathagata said, "Gopa, I am not talking about leaving you tomorrow. But there may be an opportune time in the coming weeks when it would be imperative for me to start the journey, and I want you to be mentally ready for it. Most importantly, I need your good wishes to be successful in this journey."

Yashodhara said, "Siddhartha dear, you have always my good wishes! I want you to do great things for the world! I am not that selfish to keep you bound to me, and neither am I feeble to be unable to take care of myself and Rahula. Be assured of that. Let us make the best of the times that we have together now with Rahula!"

Tathagata was very happy to hear these strong and loving words from his dear wife and said, "Gopa, I will be always indebted to you. You are a shining light!"

A couple of months passed since Tathagata had the above discussions with his parents and Yashodhara. The day of *Vaisakha Poornima* was approaching. He knew in his mind that it was an auspicious day in his life. He wanted to start the big journey for the unknown on that day itself.

On the day before *Vaisakha Poornima*, Tathagata told his parents and Yashodhara that he would be visiting Lumbini Gardens in the morning, to commemorate his birth there twenty-nine years back. He asked Channa to keep the horse ready for a ride to Lumbini Gardens very early in the morning so that they could come back to Kapilvastu before the summer sun was too high. Yashodhara packed some essential things for him to take for the journey in the morning. He had dinner with his parents and Yashodhara early that evening. Rahula also was there eating tits and bits with them and brightening the environment. Tathagata barely slept that night. He held Yashodhara close to him for the whole night. He kissed her again and again as if he had not seen her for a long time. Perhaps the silence between them told volumes about the storm to come. He held Rahula on one side and kissed him again and again. Some hours after midnight, he abruptly got up to get ready for the journey ahead. It took him some time to get ready for this trip at that time of the night since he had to make sure that no one was disturbed from sleep. Finally, he was ready. He took a final glance at sleeping Yashodhara and Rahula and left for the downstairs. Channa was waiting with the horse at the door. They mounted on the horse without much talk and off they went galloping towards the city gate on the east side of Kapilvastu. The gates were made open as the guards had been earlier notified of their planned ride early in the morning. They started their journey on the road towards Lumbini Gardens.

They reached Lumbini Gardens well past the sunrise. Tathagata went near the *Sala* tree and sat down to meditate on the recollection of his late mother Queen Maya. He asked for her blessings too. Soon he was ready to start his new journey to the unknown!

He told Channa that they would be going in the southeast direction towards Magadha country instead of turning back to Kapilvastu and that he would tell him the reason once they arrived at their target area. They continued forward and reached the border of Shakya country after a couple of hours. Crossing the river Rohini, they moved into the state of the Koliyas. They kept their southeast march towards Magadha and reached river Anoma. Crossing the river Anoma, they reached the country of the Mallas. Nearby was the village of Anupriya in the Malla Republic. He told Channa there to turn back and go to Kapilvastu along with the horse Kanthaka. Tathagata said, "Channa, I am becoming a *Sharamana* and abandoning my householder status from today. I had already discussed this with my parents and Yashodhara."

With that, Tathagata took out his sword and cut down his long hair. He took out the princely dress from his body and gave it to Channa along with all the ornaments he had. He wore a yellow robe that he had brought along with him, just one that befits a *Shramana*. He told Channa, "Please go back and give these ornaments and dresses to my parents and say that I have left home to become a *Shramana* in the quest for solutions to life's sufferings. I would be back to Kapilvastu to share, if and when I find the truth."

Channa begged repeatedly to be allowed to follow him. Tathagata told him not to and said, "Channa, you have been a good friend to me. From today on, I am completely free and I belong to the whole world. I will always remember the services you have rendered me. Go back my friend, take good care of Kanthaka, and convey my messages to my parents and Yashodhara."

Tathagata said goodbye to Kanthaka, his dear horse and companion of the youth. He said goodbye to Channa and started walking towards the village of Anupriya.

●●●

Tathagata cuts off hair and says goodbye to Channa

-11-

The Wandering Monk

It was a bright late morning sun shining on the sands of river Anoma. Tathagata could see a mango grove at a distance. He hastened to walk up the hill on the river bed towards that direction. He had filled up his *Kamandalu* with the water from the river. It was a relief when he reached the cool shade of the mango grove. He sat down and had a gulp of water to extinguish his thirst. As he rested there, he was elated to see two *Shramanas* coming towards the grove from the village side. When they approached him, he introduced himself, "Respected Sir, I am Siddhartha Gautama from Kapilvastu. I just left home to become a *Shramana* in search of truth. Are there any masters around here who could help me to go in the right direction?"

The older of the *Shramanas* said, "We are from the hermitage of Bhriguputra at Anupriya. You can come with us and find out for yourself. Just wait for some moments while we pluck out some of the mangoes and then we can all go back together".

So, Tathagata went to the hermitage of Bhriguputra, accompanied by the *Shramana*. He saw many *Shramanas* and householders performing different penances, each one displaying some type of pain and hardship. It was assumed that the harsher the pain and the discomfort, the more was the merit credited towards the *moksha*. Some stood in the hot sun for hours together, with only one foot on the ground. Many stood submerged for long hours while the water was up to their necks. Many of them ate uncooked food, such as leaves, roots, and fruits that were collected from the fields and the jungles. All of them consumed as little quantity as possible so that they could sustain their bodies and carry out other regular activities. Everyone had the goal of achieving happiness here on the earth itself while they were still alive. They also wanted to reach the heavens after their death or be reborn in the image of the gods. What a scene of misery and hope intermixed!

At that moment in his life, Tathagata did not see how these acts led to happiness on this earth or in the heavens later. In any case, he knew that it was not going to lead him to nirvana or the cessation of the cycle of birth. So, he only spent some nights in that hermitage and decided to go to Vaishali, the old capital of Kosala country and the present capital of Vrije's Federation. He came to know that Vaishali was surrounded by *ashrams* of many famous gurus and one of them was that of sage Arada Kalama.

As Tathagata was preparing to leave for Vaishali, he met two emissaries from Kapilvastu sent by his father Raja Suddhodana. One of them was a minister in the assembly and the other was one of the palace staff. The palace staff informed Tathagata of the sad conditions in the palace, "Your mother Queen Prajapati, and Princess Yashodhara have not stopped crying until now. Your son Rahula is always searching for you. There is a feeling of abandonment in Rahula's face. Your father is the one who is stricken with grief and has not come out of the palace at all. He asked us to go immediately and to persuade you and bring you back to Kapilvastu."

The minister addressed Tathagata and said, "The king is very sad. He wanted to give up the mantle of kingship in your favor, whenever you would want. The people of Kapilvastu looked towards you to provide leadership and to give them the right advice during the time of crisis in the state. Every one of the members in the assembly praised your wisdom and vision for the peace and prosperity of Kapilvastu. Why do you want to disappoint your family members and the people? Your return to Kapilvastu would be the greatest merit you could do for this world! Please reconsider your decision and come back. You can perform all of the religious ceremonies in search of deliverance while staying as a householder with your family members at your own home. Many of the royal *Rishis* of the past had their deliverance while ruling the country at the same time. They are examples for you to follow."

Tathagata was even more determined now, compared to when he left home, to continue his search for the truth, and he said, "How can I re-enter the burning house that I abandoned until I find the truth? I would surely come back to Kapilvastu, if and when I find the truth. I would then share my findings with my family members and the people of Kapilvastu. Please tell the king not to grieve for me anymore, and wish me success in my search." Thus, Tathagata persuaded the two emissaries from his father to go back to Kapilvastu and not follow him any further.

From Anupriya, Tathagata went to the city of Vaishali looking for the hermitage of sage Arada Kalama. Vaishali was the capital of the Lichchavis Republic and also the center of Vrije's Federation of the adjoining eight republics. Hence, it was a very important cultural and political center. Once

Tathagata entered the hermitage, he introduced himself to the hermit, "I am Siddhartha Gautama from Kapilvastu. I have recently left my family to become a *Shramana*. I am searching for the truth behind the sufferings of the world. I would like to be your disciple and learn from you the paths to deliverance. Would you please accept me?"

Sage Arada marveled at Tathagata's strong resolve and determination to renounce the good life during the prime of his youth. Sage Arada said, "I do usually investigate and then accept. But you seem to be so firm and resolute. Hence, I agree to accept you as a disciple right away. Study with me as you wish and I would not conceal anything from you." Tathagata was overjoyed and thought that he had now someone, who could guide him through the difficult path of ascetic life.

Sage Arada explained his philosophy in the following ways. "You reach the highest level of happiness when you become free from the passions that afflict you. When you restrain your sense organs, renounce all evil, and then strive for the tranquility of the mind, all interfering thoughts disappear from your mind. Your mind becomes completely quiet and it brings forth joy and happiness. You then reach the first stage of contemplation. One develops many likes and dislikes over the years due to discriminatory reasoning. When you avoid both the desires and the dislikes, you attain the second state of contemplation. You feel a deep level of emotional joy at that time. You may think that to be a stage of liberation since both the pleasures and the pains have been left behind and you are set free! You further concentrate and proceed this way to reach your goals."

Tathagata learned the meditation skills quickly at the hermitage. He closely observed the ways of other disciples and ensured that his practice was thorough. Soon he understood the teachings of sage Arada completely and did enough practice to master them. He told the sage about his achievement. The sage commended him for his quick attainment of the meditative states and said, "You have great will, concentration, mindfulness, and wisdom to succeed as an ascetic. You have achieved the meditative states in a very short time and know as much now from the experience you had here. I invite you to join me in leading the school. Together, we can attract a large number of disciples, and hence we would be very successful and profitable. Of course, we would be very helpful to the seekers too."

Tathagata thought that sage Arada's teachings led one to the sphere of 'nothingness' or 'emptiness' since one had emptied all his likes and dislikes, was free from the passions, and had developed his concentration further to feel part of the infinite space. But this did not lead to cessation of suffering or gain of any new knowledge. Why should Tathagata stop there in his quest when he had left behind his family, wealth, and power? So, he said, "Revered Arada, I am deeply obliged to you for allowing me to learn and master your meditation techniques. But I must continue my search for deliverance from the sufferings due to old age, death, and disease!"

So, Tathagata left the hermitage of sage Arada in search of a teacher who would lead him further on the path to freedom from old age, death, and disease. He came to know that there were a few *ashrams* in the hills around Rajagriha, the capital of Magadha. One such *ashram* was that of Rudraka Ramaputra and he wanted to go there. So, he went further southwest from Vaishali, crossed the river Ganga, and finally reached Rajagriha.

Tathagata was pleasantly surprised to see the beautiful

palatial buildings at Rajagriha. He got the occasion to see from the front of the palace the King of Magadha while he was walking on the main street of Rajagriha. He accepted alms at the few places on the street and then retired to the hilly area on the outskirts of the city. As he was resting there, Bimbisara, the King of Magadha, came there accompanied by a few of his attendants. The king had seen from his terrace Tathagata walking down the main street past his palace and was curious about the unusual *Shramana*, who was drawing everyone's attention on the street. So, he had sent one of his people to follow Tathagata to the hills and then to report to him.

King Bimbisara came to meet Tahagata at the place where he was resting after eating the food that was donated during the collection of alms around the city. After introductions, the king sat down on the rock next to Tathagata and said, "I have a strong friendship with your family, and hence I am pained to see you in the saffron dress and walking down the street collecting alms. You are so young to discard the pleasures of life and follow a mendicant's life. If religion is your main aim, you can always follow your royal ancestors. They had achieved their goals by performing penances and sacrifice while staying with the family and contributing to everyone's happiness!"

Tathagata understood the genuine concerns shown towards him by King Bimbisara. So, he said, "I appreciate your gesture of friendship and concern towards me and my family. I am in search of deliverance from the sufferings due to old age, disease, and death. Pleasures and pains are always mixed. Even a king endures various troubles for the sake of his people. I am looking for a world where there is no disease, no old age, no birth, no death, and no fear. How can I wait till old age, when I do not know when death will come? I have come to Rajagriha to meet seer Rudraka Ramaputra. He is proclaimed to have teachings that lead one to liberation. So, O! king, guard best your country and preserve the peace, tranquility, and happiness for your people. Please hold your religion high and excuse my words that may sound harsh. I am speaking from the bottom of my heart and I sincerely thank you for your concerns."

The young king folded his hands at Tathagata and said, "Please remember me to share your findings, once you reach your goals". Tathagata said, "Definitely, O! King, I would never forget your friendly concerns and would be back to see you!"

Tathagata arrived at the hermitage of sage Rudraka Ramaputra and introduced himself. Sage Rudraka had learned his techniques from his father Rama. Sage Rudraka taught many of the ideas from the early Upanishads, such as Chandogya Upanishad. One key concept was the doctrine of Brahman, the ultimate reality, being present in all the things in the universe. The reflection of Brahman in the individual was called Atman and that was equivalent to the concept of an immortal soul present in every living being.

Sage Rudraka said his teachings led one to see things as they were. It also helped one perceive what one did not see explicitly. Take the case of the well-sharpened razor; people can see the razor, but cannot see the sharpened edge, since it is too fine. Similarly, one may not be able to see it, but one can perceive the Atman, which is within every living being.

Sage Rudraka also taught meditation to his students and led them through the different meditation stages. Tathagata quickly acquired all the required meditation skills in the *ashram*. He was able to experience the state of 'neither consciousness nor nonconsciousness' that sage Rudraka taught. This was the highest state of formless dhyana (*Arupa dhyana*). One first completes the four states of meditations on material or mental objects (*Rupa dhyana*) and then only one goes through the four states of formless dhyana:

1. Meditation on the realm of infinity of space,
2. Meditation on the realm of infinity of consciousness,
3. Meditation on the realm of nothingness,
4. Meditation on the realm of neither consciousness nor unconsciousness.

The state of neither consciousness nor unconsciousness was just a step ahead of the state of 'no-thingness' or 'emptiness' that Tathagata had achieved earlier in the *ashram* of sage Arada Kalama. When he reported to sage Rudraka about his achievements, he commended him for his quick learning and readily offered him the stewardship of the school. Sage Rudraka said that it was his father Rama who had realized and proclaimed the realm of neither consciousness nor unconsciousness. He had not realized it and hence Tathagata was ahead of him. He said that he was old now and would prefer someone young and capable like Tathagata to take over the stewardship of the school.

Since he was ready to hand over the entire leadership of the school, Tathagata felt very honored at this request. But he realized that there was no ultimate insight into the sufferings of the world and enlightenment. So, he thought that he had to keep up his search for deliverance from the suffering due to old age, disease, and death. So far, he had not got any new knowledge about the problems of the sufferings, he only had learned different meditation techniques. He did not think it was right to trap himself as the head of a religious school and abandon his original mission. Hence, Tathagata left the hermitage of sage Rudraka Ramaputra in search of enlightenment.

Tathagata had so far taken the guidance of two masters, Arada Kalama and Rudraka Ramaputra. He certainly learned a lot more about the meditative states. However, he had not solved the problem of unending rebirth and consequent suffering. Neither did he get any extra knowledge or wisdom about the root cause of the suffering in the world. So, he had to march further in his search, but it had to be now with efforts and guidance from within himself!

●●●

-12-

Enlightenment at Uruvilva

After completing the training at the hermitage of sage Rudraka Ramaputra, Tathagata searched for a peaceful place, where he could strive towards his goals through his efforts. He went further southwest from Rajagriha and came upon an area called Uruvilva on the side of the river Niranjana. There were a few villages around Uruvilva, and one of them was a township called Senanigrama, where the army commander and the members of Magadha army resided. On the bank of the river, he found a beautiful spot where there was a peaceful and pleasant grove. He could easily seek alms in the morning for his daily food intake since the villages were not very far from that spot. So, Tathagata decided that to be the most auspicious place for starting his new tryst by focusing on his efforts.

While staying at Uruvilva, Tathagata came upon five disciples of sage Rudraka Ramaputra. They had earlier taken training under sage Rudraka and were working on further progress through their individual efforts. But they were all staying together as a group for convenience and support from each other. They were performing different austerities while staying around the area in Uruvilva. They were trying to attain their deliverance or *Moksha* by employing different meditation techniques. Simultaneously, they also controlled the amount of food intake and the breathing process. They were Kaundanya, Bhadriya, Vappa, Mahanama, and Aswajit. These five ascetics admired Tathagata's strong determination and continuous efforts to search for the truth. Hence, they joined him in the common search for *Moksha*. They looked towards him as the leader of the group who would lead from the front and set examples for the group. They had also vowed that whoever first arrived at the truth, would share that with the others in the group.

The group had a belief that they could purify themselves and achieve their final deliverance by continuous self-mortification. They tried to subdue and control the body by taking the least amount of food while releasing the mind by simultaneously employing meditation techniques. Tathagata was the most zealous of the group in adopting the strenuous self-mortification regimen to control the body. Since he had already tried the yoga techniques at sage Arada Kalama and the Upanishadic teachings and meditation steps at sage Rudraka Ramaputra, Tathagata was in favor of experimenting with the ascetic methods along with the other five members of the group.

For Tathagata, the initial period of staying alone near the forest was a very difficult challenge. The loneliness of the forest was a very hard thing to get used to. Until that time in life, Tathagata was never that much alone throughout the day and the night. He had never spent any time alone in a forest, staying away far from the people and the villages and the towns. He would often not meet any of his ascetic companions for days together. He could only hear the chirping of the birds or the sounds made by the animals.

The nights in the forest were even more frightening. Tathagata was full of fear whenever he heard any kind of sound, either from an animal passing by or a bird making any special sound. Even the wind rustling through the branches of the trees near his shelter would often evoke tremendous fear in him. It took some time for Tathagata to get used to this sort of total silence and loneliness. He had to resort to very hard mental self-discipline to control his fear and keep his mind cool during the nights so that he could pursue his goals in the deep darkness and silence.

Tathagata tried to experiment with many different ascetic yogic practices. He tried to get an understanding of the problems of life by forcing his mind to stay focused on a particular situation and then he tried to get some insights from that experience. He would be able to subdue his mind finally after considerable efforts. But then, he would have no insight or definite conclusion regarding the problem at hand. After a while, it became clear to Tathagata that that sort of forcing the mind was not very conducive to a full understanding of the problem or getting any solution to the problem.

Tathagata also tried non-breathing meditation techniques by holding breathing for as long as possible, while practicing trance. He did not arrive at any special knowledge or insight with those experiments, but rather he got sharp pains all over his entire body. There were headaches and stomach cramps too. Tathagata was forced to abandon all those methods.

As the next step, Tathagata reduced the amount of food consumed daily. He accepted no foods that were brought to him and begged for alms only once a week. Many times, he only ate leaves, roots, wild fruits, and vegetables. Thus, he steadily reduced food. He did not cut his hair and beard. He wore rags and slept in the cremation grounds. He spent the hot summer days in the sun. He went through the cold nights of the winter without any clothes. As a result of all of these rigorous self-mortification practices, much beyond what other companions did, his body became extremely frail, with all limbs and not much flesh anymore.

Since Tathagata took so little food for quite some time, the body reached a state of extreme emaciation. His limbs became like the dry and knotted joints of a dried bamboo tree. His buttocks looked like a camel's hoof. His spine could be seen along with its protruding vertebra. His ribs looked like the exposed rafters of a house. His pupils sunk deep in their sockets. His scalp dried up and shriveled like a dried-up bitter gourd. When he touched his skin on the belly, he almost touched his backbone, because he had become too thin and his front and back had come very close to each other. If he passed excrement or urine, he fell over on his face. If he rubbed his limbs, rotted hair came away in his hand.

Tathagata struggled for years by experimenting with those most rigorous ascetic practices. Finally, he came very close to death's door, rather than getting closer to the goals he had set when he started the journey from his home and family. Once, when he was taking a bath in the river Niranjana, his feeble body was almost swept away, but somehow, he clung to a tree branch and slowly got up from the water and then fell unconscious on the ground at the river bank. Sujata, the daughter of the village elder, fortunately, saw him lying there. She was carrying rice milk to offer the deity. She fed the rice milk through Tathagata's mouth, and thus he regained consciousness and stayed alive.

After that incident, Tathagata realized the futility of the ascetic practices of torturing the body to gain an understanding of the truth. He searched for the right paths to achieve his goal of enlightenment and understood that the right path to liberation was a middle path between the two extremes of a luxurious life catering excessively to the five senses and that of a life of self-mortification. To think free and live free, one must not resort to any of the two extreme paths, where the senses control you completely. One must tread on the middle path satisfying the basic wants of life, and then carry on the meditational and mind-based techniques to gain enlightenment. At that time, he remembered the peaceful meditational state he had gained in his childhood under the rose-apple tree, at the time of the plowing ceremony in Kapilvastu. He thought that to be the most appropriate path to enlightenment. With a weakened body, he could never hope to succeed in gaining enlightenment. So, he completely discarded his practice of self-mortification and started taking normal food. His emaciated body regained its health gradually and he fully recovered his physical and mental vigor.

The five accompanying Bhikshus who lived around him in Uruvilva were very disappointed with his changed attitude in accepting the normal food. They thought that he had abandoned the path to enlightenment and had gone back towards a life of abundance. So, they left Tathagata alone in Uruvilva and went away to pursue their goals elsewhere near Varanasi.

Tathagata was undaunted though in his determination to search for the truth. He kept on striving towards his goals while living alone in Uruvilva without the companionship of the five ascetics. Days and months passed by and he kept on his quest.

It was the day of *Vaisakha Poornima* and Tathagata had a cool bath in the river Niranjana. He then came and sat down cross-legged under the Pipal tree and vowed not to rise again, until he attained full enlightenment. He was utterly determined in his efforts to realize the truth – the complete truth behind life's suffering, disease, and death.

Tathagata kept the focus of his attention on the breathing in and breathing out process. He practiced awareness of the breathing process and brought down the breathing in and out to a very fine rhythmic state. He slowly entered the first meditative stage of absorption by quieting his mind. His whole body felt immersed in a deep sense of delight and pleasure because of the state of intense concentration that he had achieved. He observed the ecstasy of his state of absorption.

Tathagata then ceased all of the reasoning and discriminating thoughts, while still concentrating on the awareness of the breathing process. He entered the second meditative stage of absorption by shifting his attention from physical pleasure to emotional pleasure. It was now a much more soothing joy that permeated his whole body.

Further increasing his concentration, he shifted from emotional pleasure to contentment, as if he had controlled the volume of his emotional pleasure. Thus, he entered upon the third meditative stage of absorption, and his body permeated with quiet contentment.

He then refined his contentment to quiet stillness and dwelt with equanimity towards joy or sorrow, negative or positive feeling either in the body or mind. He entered upon the fourth meditative stage of absorption. There was no pleasure and pain with the purity of mindfulness and equanimity, there was only deep peacefulness.

Now that he had gone through all four stages of absorptions related to form or *Rupa dhyana*, he attempted to go through the stages of *Arupa dhyana*. He moved to the fifth meditative stage of absorption by contemplating himself in an infinite space. He focused his attention on his body and mentally expanded his sphere infinitely outward in the space. He was still conscious of himself.

Further increasing his concentration, he gazed at infinite spaciousness by mentally realizing infinite consciousness. He thus moved to the sixth meditative stage of absorption by shifting his attention to infinite consciousness. He felt one with the whole universe.

He reached the seventh meditative stage of absorption by shifting his attention to the content of consciousness and realized that there was no perception of diversity and that the contents of infinite consciousness were devoid of any permanent nature, that all the things in the world were devoid of intrinsic existence. It was a feeling of nothingness.

He then moved to the eighth meditative stage of absorption, by letting go of his feeling of nothingness. This was a very peaceful state, where there was neither perception nor non-perception. He rested in a calm quiet state.

Once he had thus purified his mind and had reached a state of pure mindfulness, and then moved through the stages of formless absorptions, he turned his attention to the recollection of previous existences. This was the first watch of the night (6 PM to 10 PM). He remembered many of his previous life stories, from birth to death. He remembered his previous names, his family, and his way of life. He recalled how he died and came back to life again.

He gained an understanding of the law of causality or Karma during the middle watch of the night (10 PM to 2 PM). According to the law of Karma, every act, good or evil, potentially lives in this world, and at the proper time, this moral energy germinates into a full-blown activity. For example, good wholesome deeds are followed by a good rebirth, and bad or unwholesome deeds are followed by an evil rebirth. He saw how sentient beings vanish and are reborn again. He saw individuals, high and low, and how each obtained according to his Karma a favorable or painful rebirth.

In the last watch of the night (2 AM to 6 AM), Tathagata focused on understanding the problem of suffering that tormented him all through the years. He understood that the mind was a repository of all the experiences, pleasant or unpleasant. One hankers after getting pleasant experiences and this is called craving for things and events. One tries to avoid unpleasant experiences and develops an aversion towards those things and events. Just as a doctor analyzed the symptoms, causes, and remedies for the disease, Tathagata viewed the problem of suffering as a disease and realized that the disease could be avoided if the cause of the disease was eliminated. He further understood that craving was at the root of the suffering and that by stopping craving, suffering would also cease. He also came upon a path to follow to stop craving, and that was the path leading to the cessation of suffering. Consequently, Tathagata formulated the following understanding of the truths operating in the universe:

1. **That life is full of suffering in the world.** Birth, old age, death, disease, disappointment, separation, etc., all involve suffering.
2. **That the cause of suffering is craving.** Attachments to people, events, and things lead to suffering. Cravings for happiness, luxury, and wealth cause suffering. Clinging to desires is at the heart of rebirth, and the consequent new cycle of old age and death.
3. **That cessation of suffering is possible.** If the

desires are controlled with a feeling of complete non-attachment, then suffering is avoided.

4. **That one has to follow the Eightfold Path for the cessation of suffering:**
   - **Right Understanding** (*Samyak Dristi*)
   - **Right Intention** (*Samyak Sankalpa*)
   - **Right Speech** (*Samyak Vachana*)
   - **Right Action** (*Samyak Karma*)
   - **Right Livelihood** (*Samyak Jivika*)
   - **Right Effort** (*Samyak Prayatna*)
   - **Right Mindfulness** (*Samyak Smriti*)
   - **Right Concentration** (*Samyak Samadhi*)

Tathagata clearly understood that the Eightfold Path was the way for the individual to adopt and practice. Now he realized that human beings would turn away from evil deeds if they saw the results of those deeds. The craving for pleasure leads one to the thirst for existence and hence one takes up new birth. Once this ignorance is removed, there is no more craving and hence no more birth and death. One achieves the state of nirvana.

Tathagata called the above "The Four Noble Truths" and realized that a clear understanding of these truths was at the heart of achieving happiness in life. Tathagata felt then that he had no more cravings or aversions. He had dispelled the darkness of ignorance and achieved the purity of mind. He had obtained the supreme security from the bondage of *Samsara* by attaining nirvana, where there was no birth, no ailing, no sorrow, and no death. Tathagata had attained enlightenment!

Tathagata was utterly elated at the gaining of the above sets of understanding during the course of the night while being at the highest level of absorption. When he saw the morning star in the sky, he felt he was the morning star. He had become one with the universe! He happily cried out:

> "A great new beginning today!
> Wandered countless births and deaths,
> But never knew the builder of the house.
> That life is too much suffering and pain!
>
> Finally, I have discovered,
> The things inside and out,
> Never to build a house anymore,
> All the building blocks are broken.
>
> Feel no pain, do not seek the pleasures,
> All my cravings have disappeared,
> See the path, clear and sublime.
> I have now attained enlightenment!
>
> I am one with the universe,
> I am the earth and the water,
> I am the morning star!
> I am the Buddha, the Enlightened one!"

Tathagata stayed put for the next seven days around the Pipal tree meditating and embellishing the enlightenment that he had achieved. He knew that all his cravings were gone forever. Although his physical body would be subject to disease and old age, he would never feel the suffering. He had achieved nirvana and would live henceforth only to deliver his messages to the people of the world so that they too could escape from their sufferings. He had finally arrived at that goal he had set when he left his home more than six years back.

During this time when Tathagata was at Uruvilva, two merchants from Uttara Utkala, Trapusha, and Bhallika stopped by one day near the Pipal tree. They were passing through that way with their caravan of carts and offered him sweets and milk to eat. He did not reveal to them his findings of the path of enlightenment but talked about his meditational experiences. They were just very happy to have met him and wanted his blessings. So, he blessed them and they became his first lay disciples.

Tathagata started thinking about whom and how he should deliver his findings. He remembered Rudraka Ramaputra but realized that he had recently died. So was Arada Kalama. Both of these teachers of his would have been so happy to receive him and his findings!

Finally, Tathagata decided that he should seek out the five companion ascetics, who had left him earlier and were staying at Rishi Patana near Varanasi. As per their earlier mutual pact, he had to disclose to them his findings regarding the cessation of suffering and the path to enlightenment. So, he started planning a trip to Varanasi to meet those earlier companions, who would be the first ones to hear his findings of the truths.

•••

-13-

Messages at Varanasi

Tathagata's enlightenment experience was so wonderful that he was just immersed in enjoying its sweetness for a few days. Finally, he started on his way to Varanasi on foot. It would take him many days to walk this distance. On his way to Gaya from Uruvilva, he met the Brahman Upaka, who was leading an ascetic life in the quest for enlightenment.

Upaka said, "Friend, your face looks so radiant and your faculties seem so clear! Who do you have as your teacher?"

Tathagata replied, "I have achieved victory over the sufferings of the world. All my cravings are gone. I have gained knowledge about the right path in life. I have achieved nirvana. I am the enlightened one, the light into the world! I am on my way to Kasi - to preach my doctrine." Hearing this, Upaka haughtily said, "It may be so, my friend!" He took a different sideway road ahead and disappeared.

From Gaya, Tathagata went to Rajagriha and then to Pataligrama on the bank of river Ganga. After crossing the river, he kept on walking on the northern shore of the river and reached the deer park in Rishi Patana, also called Isipatana, north of Varanasi.

The five monks, who had lived at Uruvilva earlier, saw him coming as he approached them. It seemed they had decided after seeing him not to accord any special respect because he lived in a state of abundance according to them. But as Tathagata came nearer, one of them took his bowl, another provided him water to wash his feet and the other prepared a seat for him. They said, "Gautama, our friend, please sit down."

Hearing this Tathagata told them, "Monks, please do not address me as 'Friend Gautama'. Now, I am an Arhat who has achieved nirvana. I have achieved victory over the sufferings of the world and have gained knowledge about the right paths to be followed in life. If you follow my instructions, you can also attain enlightenment."

The monks said, "You had abandoned the path of self-mortification that led to enlightenment and had chosen the path of abundance. How can you claim to have acquired such knowledge?"

Tathagata replied, "Monks, I did not live a life of abundance or a life of self-mortification. I achieved enlightenment by meditating under the Pipal tree, day and night, and for weeks and months. I will instruct you, why and how to practice the Dharma."

"The path of passions, luxury, and indulgence in vulgar entertainment is to be avoided. Similarly, you should avoid the path of self-torture, useless penances, and painful practices. The right path is the middle way, not the path of opulence or penury, but a middle path that brings in calmness and leads to proper insight and ultimately to enlightenment!"

"Oh monks, remember the First Noble Truth that life is full of sufferings: birth is suffering, old age is suffering, death is suffering, and so are disappointments, defections, separations, and diseases."

"Oh monks, the Second Noble Truth of the cause of suffering is the craving. It is craving that leads to rebirth and the associated cycle of suffering during life. It is the craving for passions, pleasures, and riches that causes suffering."

"Oh monks, the Third Noble Truth is that the cessation of sufferings occurs at the abandonment of the cravings, the complete non-attachment to things and sentient beings."

"Oh monks, the Fourth Noble Truth is that the Eightfold Path leads to the elimination of the cravings, which in turn leads to the cessation of suffering. The Eightfold Path is to be followed by an individual who wants deliverance from the sufferings."

"The first part of the path is *Samyak Dristi* or Right Understanding, whereby one understands what are wholesome deeds and unwholesome deeds. One comprehends the law of Karma and the Four Noble Truths: that there is suffering, there is a cause of the sufferings, and that the cessation of suffering can occur by following the Eightfold Path".

"The second part of the path is *Samyak Sankalp* or Right Aspiration, whereby one avoids any greed, harbors no hatred, and keeps no delusion".

"The third part of the path is *Samyak Vachana* or Right Speech, whereby one communicates no false or malicious speech, delivers no harsh word and does no idle chatter about others".

"The fourth part of the path is *Samyak Karma* or Right Action, whereby one does no killing of sentient beings, does not steal what belongs to others, and performs no sexual misconduct".

"The fifth part of the path is *Samyak Jivika* or Right

Livelihood, whereby one does not adopt the wrong or corrupt means of livelihood, such as armaments business, animals trade, flesh trade, etc."

"The sixth part of the path is *Samyak Prayatna* or Right Effort, whereby one abandons all unwholesome states, such as entertaining bad thoughts, and one sustains wholesome thoughts, such as creating good thoughts while controlling the senses".

"The seventh part of the path is *Samyak Smriti* or Right Mindfulness, whereby one rightly contemplates on one's body, feelings, mind, and objects of mind".

"The eighth part of the path is *Samyak Samadhi* or Right Concentration, whereby one abandons lust, ill-will, sloth, worry and doubt and focuses on attaining wisdom".

"Oh monks, you have to fully comprehend these Four Noble Truths and then abandon your cravings and realize the cessation of pain by practicing the Eightfold Path. You have to follow all eight parts of the path concurrently. This will lead to your enlightenment and nirvana. The knowledge of these Noble Truths was not known or heard before and I acquired this while passing through my enlightenment process. I am now the Buddha, the enlightened one and you all have to address me and treat me as such."

The five disciples Kaundinya, Bhadriya, Vappa, Mahanama, and Aswajit listened very attentively to these instructions given by Tathagata. They realized that the explanations and remedies for the seekers of ultimate happiness or 'Moksha' were logical, coherent, and as per the highest moral laws of the time. All five of them realized that Tathagata indeed had achieved enlightenment. They fell at the feet of Tathagata and requested him to accept them as his disciples.

Tathagata uttered, "Come in Bhikshus", and each of them uttered the three refuges:

"Buddham Sharanam Gachhami.
Dharmam Sharanam Gachhami.
Sangham Sharanam Gachhami."

Thus started the *Bhikshu* Sangha with the first five disciples on the day of *Asadha Poornima,* the full moon day of the rainy period. Tathagata told the disciples that each of them could achieve nirvana if they followed the Dharma diligently and with an open mind. It could take days, months, and years depending upon the personal background and efforts.

Tathagata stayed with the five disciples at Rishi Patana to further train the disciples in meditation and carrying out daily routines as per the Dharma.

It was now appropriate for Tathagata to further explain to his disciples the three marks of Existence or *Trilakshana* that apply to all the sentient beings: 1) Impermanence or *Anitya,* 2) Suffering or *Duhkha,* and 3) No-self or *Anatman.* That all things are impermanent and hence in a state of flux. That all beings go through suffering and that all beings are devoid of soul or *Atman.* An understanding of these three aspects of existence is essential in the removal of suffering.

Tathagata again emphasized that there was no permanent soul that transmigrated from one life to another. Then, how do you define a living being? Tathagata explained that all sentient beings constitute five *Skandhas* or aggregates that together describe their different aspects: 1. Name and Form or *Nama-Rupa,* 2. Sensation or *Vedana,* 3. Perception or *Sanjna,* 4. Mental formations or *Samskaras,* and 5. Consciousness or *Vijnana.*

The first aggregate is name and form. The existence

associated with form has six sense organs: eye, ear, nose, tongue, body, and mind. The second aggregate that defines a sentient being is its feeling or sensation. The third aggregate is one's conception or mental power through which he creates a mental picture of things. The fourth aggregate is the total storage of information regarding past experiences of events and entities, their pleasantness and unpleasantness. The fifth aggregate is one's consciousness and there are six different types of consciousness corresponding to the six sense organs and their respective processes: seeing, hearing, smelling, taste, touch, and thinking.

Everyone should understand the law of Karma. It is the law of causality, whereby every action of the individual has effects on that individual and the world. Good institutions and deeds contribute to the future good karma and happiness.

Tathagata and the five disciples stayed put at Rishi Patana since it was the rainy season now and it was customary at the time not to travel during *Varsha* or the rainy season. They used this time to hold more deep discussions and intense training sessions.

During this time, Tathagata further discussed the interdependency of everything in the world. Tathagata explained that all phenomena arose in dependence upon other pre-existing phenomena only. There was thus dependent origination or dependent arising only. Nothing had an independent self or essence. This was called conditioned arising. There could be a chain of events acting as a chain of conditioning or links dependent on each other which lead to certain subsequent conditions. Thus, *Bhava Chakra* or Wheel of Life is explained in terms of the twelve *Nidana* of *Pratityasamutpada*, meaning twelve links of conditioned origination:

1. In the beginning, there is *Avidya* or ignorance about the Four Noble Truths, the Three Marks of Existence, the *Skandhas*, Karma, and the Wheel of Life. This results in the wrong assessment of reality because one does not know the origination and cessation of suffering, nor the practice leading to the cessation of suffering.

2. From *Avidya* comes forth *Samskara* or volitional formations. This is manifested through body, speech, and mind, and forms the basis of our character and personal Karmic pattern.

3. From *Samskara* comes forth *Vijnana* or sense consciousness or discernment. The consciousness re-enters another womb after the death of an individual who has not been liberated, leading to the next life of the individual.

4. From *Vijnana* comes forth *Nama-Rupa* or name and form. The new empirical being is constituted of mentality and corporeality or the five *Skandhas*.

5. From *Nama-Rupa* comes forth *Sadayatana* or the six sense bases which are the six object realms of the senses: eyes, ears, nose, tongue, body, and mind. The senses present themselves to the being after its birth.

6. From *Sadayatana* comes forth *Sparsha* or interaction with its environment (sense impression).

7. From *Sparsha* comes forth *Vedana* or sensation in someone completely ignorant.

8. From *Vedana* comes forth *Trsna* or craving (desire, greed, and thirst). Kama Trsna is for sensual pleasures. *Bhava Trsna* is the desire for permanence as a being. *Bibhava Trsna* is the desire to separate from the unpleasant state.

9. From *Trsna* comes forth *Upadana* or clinging to a womb after the death.

10. From *Upadana* comes forth *Bhava* or a new existence. This refers to the new formation of Karmic tendencies. *Bhava* will come to fruition through future experiences.

11. From *Bhava* comes forth *Jati* or birth. This refers to the process of Karmic tendencies of *Bhava* coming to fruition through the birth of a new being. That which was desired and conditioned comes to be.

12. From *Jati* comes forth *Duhkha* or pain in the form of aging, decay, and death. Once the new being is born, it is inevitable for decay and death to occur. When deaths occur, there is the breakdown and dissolving of the processes for the being.

This sequence completely explains the processes related to the previous life (steps 1 and 2), the present life (steps 3 to 10), and the next life (steps 11 and 12) of a sentient being.

As one moves from one life to the next, there is no 'soul' being migrated, since there is none, but just the consciousness is transferred to a new womb. Those who eliminate the cravings attain nirvana and live with ultimate happiness in the world and do not cling to wombs as seeds when physical deaths occur. Consequently, there is no recurring life for them and they reach Pari nirvana. Thus, avoidance of birth leads to the cessation of suffering.

●●●

Tathagata giving instructions to the Five Disciples

-14-

The Dharma Spreads

Since it was the rainy season, Tathagata spent a few weeks living in the cottage at Rishi Patana deer park. It was customary for monks to stay put at one location during the rainy season lasting about three months. It is difficult to travel during this period, and one may also damage the crops and trample on the insects swimming all around the pathways. Of course, they used to go to the nearby villages and towns in the late morning along with their begging bowls to collect food for the single meal that they took every day.

It was very early in the morning one day. Tathagata was resting inside his cottage at the park. The tender rays of the sun were falling inside the cottage. He saw a young man taking a brisk walk towards the cottage. The young man came inside the cottage and paid respects to him.

He said, "Oh, Great Monk! I am Yasha from Varanasi. My father is the biggest gold jewelry merchant there. I live with my parents and wife in Varanasi, very near our business premises. I have been having a very luxurious life so far! I usually go to the music and dance programs during the day and the evening. Now I am fed up with this way of life and have come to you for your noble advice. Please help me! I have heard about you from the people. Please lead me the right way!"

Tathagata was most impressed by Yasha's sincerity and yearning for a noble path and decided then and there to reveal to him the truth that he had learned from his deep and long struggle. Tathagata said, "Yasha, sit down in front of me and I will tell you all about the Dharma, the noble path for you to take! The path pursuing the extremes of sensual pleasures, riches, and wanton extravagance, and the path of self-mortification and extreme deprivation of physical and mental pleasures are both wrong. The right path is a middle path between these two extremes. So, Yasha, prepare yourself for such a middle path!"

"Recognize the Four Noble Truths: First that there is suffering in the world, second that the suffering is due to one's craving for things, third that there is a cure from the suffering, and the fourth that the Eightfold Path will lead to a cure for suffering and final deliverance."

Tathagata explained to Yasha the Eightfold Path of Right Understanding, Right Aspiration, Right Speech, Right Action, Right Livelihood, Right Effort, Right Mindfulness, and Right Concentration.

Hearing these words, Yasha fell and touched Tathagata's feet and said, "Oh Great Sage! I seek the path shown by you and renounce the family life. Please accept me as your disciple!"

Tathagata then made Yasha say, "I take refuge in the Buddha, I take refuge in the Dharma and I take refuge in the Sangha." Yasha repeated the vows two more times and thus became the newest convert to the Dharma.

Towards the evening, Yasha's father came looking for his missing son and met Tathagata while he was strolling in the park. Yasha's father asked, "Have you seen my son

Yasha? He fled away from home the previous night and we are concerned about his whereabouts."

Tathagata told him that Yasha had indeed come there that morning in search of the cure for his suffering, and had attentively listened to his talks and had decided to forsake his householder life and become a monk in the Sangha. Yasha's father was curious to know about the Dharma, and so Tathagata explained to him about the Middle Path, the Four Noble Truths, and the Eightfold Path. He was greatly influenced by Tathagata's explanations and wanted to become a lay disciple. Thus, Yasha's father became the first lay disciple of the Sangha.

Tathagata told him of the five rules that he had to follow as an Upasaka in the Sangha: 1. Not to take any life, 2. Not to steal what is not yours, 3. Not to lie, 4. Not to have any sexual misconduct, and 5. Not to become intoxicated. Yasha's father readily agreed to these conditions and took the vows of refuge in the Buddha, the Dharma, and the Sangha.

Yasha's father had a chance now to meet all of Tathagata's six disciples including Yasha. He could see a glowing radiance of happiness on Yasha's face and knew that Yasha could not go back home to live with the family. However, he invited all seven of them to come the next day for lunch at his house in Varanasi. They gladly accepted his invitation and went there the next day for lunch. They met there Yasha's father, mother, and wife. Of course, strictly speaking, she was no longer his wife, since he had renounced the householder life and had become a monk. They all had sumptuous meals served and enjoyed the hospitality extended to them. It was time now for Tathagata to deliver a lecture on the Dharma as a way of thanking them in return for the hospitality extended. Fifty-four of

Yasha's close friends from Varanasi were also present in the audience. Tathagata told them about the Middle Path, the Four Noble Truths including the Eightfold Path.

After hearing the teaching, Yasha's mother and his wife wanted to be the lay supporters of the Dharma and thus were accepted as the first two female lay supporters or *Upasikas*. All of Yasha's fifty-four friends decided to become monks and join the Sangha. So, they had now a total of sixty monks in the Sangha.

Tathagata's main concern now was to teach these new entrants to the Sangha, so that they can attain enlightenment and be ready to spread the Dharma and be of service to others. Kaundinya, Aswajit, and Mahanama also participated in these efforts to explain the Middle Path, the Four Noble Truths including the Eightfold Path. They made them understand the impermanence of every aspect of life and that there was no basic essence or soul of either matter or beings.

It took time and effort to change the new entrants from a free life to a disciplined life of focusing only on enlightenment and living harmoniously with all the members of the Sangha. During the *Varsha* observation, the members of the Sangha did not travel and focused on spiritual discussions and intensive meditation practices.

The *Bhikshu* Sangha had sixty members now. The new monks were also shown how to make the alms rounds in the morning and how to schedule their times according to their needs. They lived and trained together at Rishi Patana. That is when they started noting down special rules of behavior for the monks. These rules for the monks were developed so that peace was maintained in the community while offering everyone an opportunity to better themselves as individuals and monks.

The remaining *Varsha* time in Rishi Patana was used to thoroughly train all the sixty members of the Sangha. It was evident to Tathagata that each of these members of the Sangha was a very important resource for spreading Tathagata's message to the neighboring communities. Yasha was a bright example of how one person could bring about a huge expansion in the Sangha. He was the reason behind the joining of fifty-four additional members into the Sangha. So, Tathagata told the monks that they should individually go to different areas of the country to spread the message of the Sangha and in the process help the people to find happiness in life.

In addition to the *Bhikshu* Sangha, Tathagata had also started the *Upasaka* Sangha when Yasha's father joined as its first member. Similarly, *Upasika* Sangha started with Yasha's mother and wife joining it. The five rules of conduct were the same for both groups. The Dharma depended largely on the support of the people, the Upasaka Sangha, and the Upasika Sangha to survive in every way.

●●●

-15-

Back to Uruvilva and Rajagriha

After about three months of observation of Varsha retreat, the rains were over. The skies were then mostly clear and one could enjoy the star-studded nights. Tathagata began his preparation to go back first to Uruvilva along with just a couple of the original five disciples. He wanted to convey his messages to the inhabitants of Uruvilva, amongst whom he had lived and struggled for six years while preparing for his enlightenment.

On the way to Uruvilva, they met a group of wealthy young men entertaining themselves along with their wives near a graveyard. One of the young men, who had no wife, had brought a courtesan as his companion. It so happened that this lady decamped with some of the valuables belonging to the group. All of them were searching for her and asked Tathagata if he had seen her.

Tathagata questioned them, "Young men, is it better for you to search for that woman or to search for your real selves?"

They all said, "It is better to search for our real selves!"

Tathagata said, "Please sit down and I will tell you all about your life in this world and how you can be free and happy."

He explained to them the Four Noble Truths and was able to convince them about the path of the Dharma. They all converted as lay followers of the Dharma.

There were three Kashyapa brothers at that time practicing special fire and water worship and maintaining long matted hair. They all lived near Uruvilva. The eldest one called Uruvilva Kashyapa had five hundred disciples. The next one called Nadi Kashyapa lived down the river Niranjana and had three hundred followers of his own. The youngest called Gaya Kashyapa lived in Gaya further down the river and had two hundred disciples.

When Tathagata arrived at Uruvilva, it was already evening time. Expecting a cold night, he went to the hermitage of Uruvilva Kashyapa and asked if he could spend the night there. Kashyapa was hesitant and said that there was a large venomous serpent that visited the grounds. Tathagata was not afraid of the serpent and spent the night there without having any problem. Later, Tathagata spent several nights in the nearby forest and used campfires in the night to ward off the animals and generate some warmth for the body.

Tathagata observed the activities of Uruvilva Kashyapa and his disciples, especially during the animal sacrifice festivity. Of course, Tathagata stayed away from his hermitage during this time, sensing that he would not like his supporters coming to these activities to be drawn to Tathagata's sphere of influence. Once, when Kashyapa boasted of his capabilities, Tathagata retorted, "Kashyapa, you are not an Arhat, and neither are you on the path to one. Your way of life is somehow incompatible with the path of an *Arhat*."

Kashyapa was somewhat surprised by this comment and fell at Tathagata's feet and said, "Please accept me as your disciple."

Tathagata said, "Kashyapa, you are the head of a group of five hundred followers. Talk to them first about the ramifications of such an event and then only I can welcome you."

Kashyapa talked with all of his followers and together they decided to become Tathagata's disciples. So, Tathagata suddenly had a total of five hundred followers at Uruvilva. Each of them shaved their head and threw away the shaved matted hair in the river, wore the yellow robes, and then took the oath to join the Sangha.

When Nadi Kashyapa and Gaya Kashyapa came to know about the conversion of their eldest brother, they also decided to join the Sangha along with their followers. So, the Sangha suddenly had more than one thousand followers in Uruvilva.

Taking all of his thousand disciples including the Kashyapa brothers, Tathagata went to Rajagriha and stayed in Latthi Vana on the day of *Pausha Poornima*, the full moon day in the winter month. When King Bimbisara of Magadha learned of Tathagata's arrival at Rajagriha, he came along with a royal retinue of courtiers, Brahmans, and other attendants to pay his respects. It had been more than seven years since they had met last at Rajagriha while Tathagata was in search of enlightenment. Now that he had achieved enlightenment and was on a mission to spread his messages to the wider world, Tathagata was ready to influence the king and seek his co-operation.

King Bimbisara was surprised to see the renowned Kashyapa brothers as Tathagata's disciples. He invited all of them to come for lunch at his palace the next day. The King said, "Respected sir, I am so happy to have your company after these years! One of my ardent wishes is to be blessed by your wisdom and that I could serve you and get to know you. Please honor me by coming to my palace tomorrow morning along with the monks and have lunch with us."

The next day King Bimbisara served with his own hands a sumptuous meal for Tathagata and the monks. There were also members of the king's family and important ministers of the court of Magadha. After the meals, Tathagata thanked the king for his hospitality and said, "Oh King! The world is full of suffering. The cause of suffering is the craving for things. There is a cure for this suffering. The cure is to tread the Eightfold Path: Right Understanding, Right Aspiration, Right Speech, Right Action, Right Livelihood, Right Effort, Right Mindfulness, and Right Concentration. Please remember that everything in this world is impermanent and that includes all sentient beings. There is no soul or Atman that is permanent having an independent existence. Everything in this world is dependent on each other. If one can understand this and follow the Eightfold Path, one can attain nirvana and be free from rebirth".

The king was very happy to hear this summary of the Dharma and wanted to be a lay follower along with the members of his family. Tathagata welcomed them all to the Sangha. King Bimbisara then donated Venu Vana, the beautiful gardens adjoining the city, for the use of the Sangha and he promised to build some shelters there for housing the monks. Thus, Tathagata started a beautiful and long chapter of association with King Bimbisara, his capital Rajagriha, and the people of Magadha.

Tathagata lived in Rajagriha for many months spreading the Dharma and introducing a large number of lay followers to the Sangha. They also had a few new monks who joined the order. Shari Putra, who was from Nalanda near Rajagriha was a follower of sage Sanjaya and once met Tathagata's disciple Aswajit during the morning period of alms. He was impressed by Aswajit and enquired about his teacher and came to Venu Vana to meet Tathagata. When Tathagata recited to him the Dharma, then and there Shari Putra decided to join the Sangha. His friend Maudgalyayana who also hailed from the surrounding area joined the Sangha as a monk. Shari Putra and Maudgalyayana became the two most revered monks in the order and helped in the spread and preservation of the Sangha.

Maha Kashyapa was another great disciple of Tathagata and he was from the village Mahatirtha in the kingdom of Magadha. He was named Pippali by his parents and hailed from a Brahman family. He was so impressed by Tathagata that he requested ordination immediately. He excelled in ascetic practices and because of his great stature in the Sangha, Tathagata had named him Maha Kashyapa to distinguish him from the Kashyapa brothers.

•••

-16-

Welcome Home to Kapilvastu

Tathagata was staying at Venu Vana located in Rajagriha. Then came Kaludayin, his boyhood playmate and the son of a courtier in his father's court at Kapilvastu. Tathagata was very happy to see someone from his city after almost seven years. He informed that Tathagata's parents were fine and that Rahula had grown to be a fine lad under the guidance of Yashodhara and the grandparents. Kaludayin said that the people of Kapilvastu had learned about the spread of the Sangha in the state of Magadha and outside. Everyone including Tathagata's parents was happy and proud that he had been successful in finding the answers to his search and that as Buddha, the awakened one, he influenced the lives of so many people. Kaludayin was very eager to learn the ways of the Dharma. So, Tathagata got him to take the vow and listen to his teachings. Kaludayin soon joined the stream and stayed at the residence of Venu Vana in Rajagriha.

One day Kaladayin requested an audience with Tathagata. It was the full moon day of the month *Phalguna* in the spring. He came and fell at Tathagata's feet and said, "Please forgive me that I did not communicate to you earlier the message that your father had sent with me. He invited you and your monks to visit Kapilavastu and bless the people with your presence. Please accept his invitation and visit Kapilavastu immediately."

It had been almost seven years since Tathagata left home in search of answers to his questions. He had left behind his aging parents, Yashodhara, and the infant son Rahula. He had walked away from twenty-nine years of his life with the people of Kapilvastu, amongst them so many of his friends and relatives. Kaludayin's message woke up Tathagata to the fact that it was time now for him to go back to Kapilvastu with his message and to soothe the wounds that resulted amongst his family and friends from that separation seven years ago.

Tathagata decided to start the journey to Kapilvastu. Kaludayin was sent ahead of him to inform Raja Suddhodana about Tathagata coming with the monks. They started the journey to Kapilvastu with five hundred monks. On the way, they stayed at Pataligrama, Vaishali, Kusinara, and Anupriya.

One late afternoon, they finally reached Nigrodha Park on the outskirts of Kapilvastu. Tathagata's father had made arrangements for them to stay there. Once people learned of their arrival, they came in droves. The next day, Tathagata finished his morning rituals and then picked up his begging bowl to go for alms. He started going from house to house from the far end of the city. The news of his accepting alms spread fast over Kapilvastu and his father came to know about it. He immediately rushed over to that lane of Kapilvastu, where Tathagata was begging for alms, and confronted him, "Siddhartha, how can you shame me by asking for alms in the very city where you grew up as a prince of opulence, and where your family distributed food and shelter to the poor of the city? As

Kshatriyas, we never engage in begging and it is not our Dharma!"

Replying to his father's comments, Tathagata said, "I did not mean to create discomfort for you, but it is our custom to beg. All of the great sages lived by obtaining food this way. All of the *Bhikshus* of our Sangha depend upon this method to get the one daily meal they are entitled to."

His father then said, "That may be your custom. But please accept my invitation to all the monks to have the meals in the palace. We would be most happy to arrange the meals inside the palace walls."

Tathagata accepted his father's invitation and they decided to have their meals inside the palace. When they arrived at the palace, they were all served a sumptuous meal. Tathagata's father and his top advisors were there, personally making sure that they were well taken care of.

The women of Kapilvastu came to greet Tathagata personally. His aunt cum foster mother Prajapati was the one most elated to see him after all these years and shed tears of joy at their meeting. Tathagata repeated the sermon to her and the assembled women. His aunt along with some other women decided then to become his lay followers.

After the meals were over, Tathagata had the chance to sit down with his father and talk to him about the Dharma. Tathagata explained to him the four truths and the principle of adopting a middle path between a luxurious opulent life and a life of self-mortification since both of these paths were wrong. Raja Suddhodana decided to be a lay follower of the Dharma. A few of the senior courtiers and relatives of Tathagata also chose to take the path of the Dharma as lay followers and became his disciples.

It was not surprising to Tathagata that Yashodhara did not come to see him. So, it was the most appropriate thing for Tathagata, after these years of separation, to go to her quarters and seek her out. No doubt, she was eager to meet with Tathagata, but her heart was heavy with emotions and love for him. Living as a monk, Tathagata had replaced his feelings of emotional love for Yashodhara with a deep sense of compassion. But in Yashodhara's world, she had years of unfulfilled and piled-up love and emotions towards Tathagata!

Tathagata went inside her chamber along with one of his chief disciples and sat down at the appointed seat waiting for her. Yashodhara came and fell near Tathagata's feet; held both of his ankles and put them on her head. Streams of tears were falling uncontrolled from her cheek, tears of joy that finally her man had come back and achieved what he longed for and that the world had recognized him as the Buddha. She was also happy that he had come back to visit Kapilvastu as he had promised and that he was spreading his message amongst the people of Kapilvastu to help them cope with the sufferings in life.

Yashodhara had so many things to tell him and ask him! But, for the moment, she was content that he was near her and that he blessed her with his message. Raja Suddhodana came to Yashodhara's chamber and talked about how she had been a follower of Tathagata all these years, "When she learned that you were only eating once a day in the morning, she also ate once and wore only yellow robes like you. She slept on the floor on top of a bamboo mat and followed all the rigors of ascetic life, although she was living here in the palace".

The following day was the celebration in honor of Tathagata's half-brother Nanda, son of his foster mother and aunt Prajapati. Nanda was two years younger than him and his age was in mid-thirty at the time. He had been married to Janapada Kalyani for some time. But he was not yet consecrated as the prince to inherit Raja Suddhodana. Now that Tathagata was visiting Kapilvastu for the first time after renouncing the householder life, Raja Suddhodana had arranged to have this celebration while Tathagata was there. There was a consecration ceremony around noon where the people of Kapilvastu were invited.

After the celebrations were completed, Nanda accompanied Tathagata to Nigrodha Park. As Tathagata enquired more about him, it came out that Nanda was ambivalent about taking the burden of the government of Kapilvastu someday. Nanda said he went through the consecration ceremony only as a formality. So, Tathagata said to Nanda, "Why don't you join the Sangha? You would be free from the cravings and the delusions of life."

Nanda said, "Yes I would like to join the Sangha as a monk". So, Tathagata ordained Nanda as a novice monk then and there. Of course, Raja Suddhodana was not very happy to learn of this. Later on, Tathagata realized that Nanda perhaps wanted to join the Sangha partly as a mark of respect for Tathagata but was attached to his wife Janapada Kalyani. So, they had to help Nanda later in the Sangha to overcome his difficulties.

Tathagata met his son Rahula on the seventh day of his stay at Kapilvastu. Yashodhara had got him into a fine dress and brought him near Tathagata at the time of meals. She had pointed at Tathagata and told Rahula that Tathagata was his father and that he should demand his inheritance from him. So, Rahula followed Tathagata after the meals and said to him, "*Shramana*, you have to give my inheritance!"

Rahula was about eight years old at the time. What inheritance could Tathagata give him as his father? The most appropriate inheritance perhaps would be to give him the happiness of life in the Sangha!

Tathagata asked his senior disciple Shari Putra to accept Rahula as a novice monk. So, Shari Putra performed the Novice Ordination or *Prabaja* on Rahula. When Raja Suddhodana learned of Rahula's ordination, he was very upset that now his grandson was also taken away to the Sangha. He talked to Tathagata and said that children should never be given novice monk ordination without getting permission from their parents. Tathagata agreed with him and they observed the rule for all future ordinations of the monks, that they must get permission from the parents and the spouses before they can be accepted as novice monks.

After a stay of about two weeks at Kapilvastu, Tathagata started his journey back to Rajagriha. On the way, they stayed at Anupriya in the Malla Republic. While they were still there, a group of seven residents from Kapilvastu met him with intentions to join the Sangha as monks. There was the barber Upali, who later rose to be the foremost expert on the laws relating to the operation of the Sangha. There were Aniruddha and Ananda, both Tathagata's paternal cousins and the sons of his father's younger brother Amitodana. There was also Devadatta, another paternal cousin and the son of his father's sister. Others who came were Bhagu, Kimbila, and Bhaddiya. The most prominent of them was Bhaddiya since his late father was a Raja ruling over the Shakyas. The seven in the group had left Kapilvastu with the intention of becoming *Shramana* and decided to join the Sangha as monks. So, Tathagata ordained all of them at Anupriya.

From Anupriya, their group went to Kaushambi, the capital of the kingdom of Vatsa. It was a prosperous trading city on the bank of river Yamuna and was connected by the trading route to Shravasti in the north and Rajagriha in the southeast. They took the routes on the side of the rivers Yamuna and Ganga to eventually reach Pataligrama on the south side of Ganga and then traveled to Rajagriha.

●●●

Tathagata and disciple in Yashodhara's Room

-17-

Shravasti and King Prasenjit

It was a few days after coming back from the trip to Kapilvastu. Tathagata was enjoying a walk early morning at Venu Vana of Rajagriha when a merchant named Sudatta came to see him. He was from Shravasti, the capital of the kingdom of Kosala, and had come there to his brother-in-law's house at Rajagriha on some business matters. It seemed that he had learned about Tathagata's presence when he enquired about the meal preparations being made at his brother-in-law's house. They had given the invitation to Tathagata and the monks for the meals that day.

Sudatta said, "Honored One, I have heard so much about you and your order, please accept me as your follower."

Tathagata readily administered the three refuge vows and Sudatta became a follower. He invited Tathagata to have a meal with him the next morning at his brother-in-law's house. They met the next day as planned and then Sudatta told him, "Honored One, I would like you to come to Shravasti. I am offering you a place for the Sangha so that you can arrange the rain retreats near Shravasti."

Tathagata gladly accepted the offer and said, "Sudatta, my only condition is that you would offer us a peaceful location!"

That was the beginning of a long association of the Sangha with Sudatta. Sudatta was also known as 'Anathapindaka' because he fed the poor of Shravasti. He was the biggest gold merchant and head of the merchant guild at Shravasti.

When Sudatta went back to Shravasti, he looked for a suitable place for the Sangha. He found on the outskirts of the city a park belonging to Prince Jeta, a brother of the King of Kosala. Prince Jeta was reluctant to sell the park to Sudatta. But Sudatta worked out a deal with the prince. He laid out on the park gold coins fully covering it as the price of the land and the prince accepted it knowing that the land would be offered as a retreat for the Sangha.

About this time at Venu Vana, came Mahali, a Lichchavis chief from Vaishali. He met Tathagata with a request on behalf of the Lichchavis of that city inviting Tathagata to visit Vaishali. They were having lots of different problems in the city at that time, including the outbreak of famines due to the lack of rain. They had sent Mahali to invite Tathagata with the hope that Tathagata would agree to visit them and bring good luck to the city. King Bimbisara was a friend of Mahali and supported this request. So, Tathagata prepared to visit Vaishali and then planned to proceed from there to Shravasti.

Tathagata set out along with two hundred of the monks. They followed the road to Pataligrama on the bank of the river Ganga. King Bimbisara also marched along with them to the shore of the Ganga. On the other side of the river, the representatives of the Lichchavis Republic were waiting to welcome Tathagata. He was then taken in a procession to Vaishali, the capital of the Lichchavis Republic. Of course, Vaishali was not new to Tathagata. He had been there for a few months at the beginning of his quest for enlightenment. When he left home, he had stopped there for instruction from guru Arada Kalama.

Vaishali was a prosperous city and the Lichchavis community selected their ruler as Raja through the council established in the city. Tathagata was warmly received at the council and had the opportunity to address the council and the inhabitants of Vaishali. He stayed a few days at Mahavana Kutagarasala on the outskirts of Vaishali. A few residents of Vaishali joined the Sangha.

Tathagata and his monks went to Shravasti from Vaishali and stayed on the outskirts of the city at Jeta Vana Park, which Anathapindaka had just acquired. The next morning, they had meals at Anathapindaka's house and he asked Tathagata, "Honored One, how do you want me to donate the park to the Sangha?"

Tathagata answered, "Sudatta, arrange such that the park would be loaned to the Sangha for the present and the future."

Thus, Anathapindaka owned the land and gave it to the Sangha for usage in perpetuity. The Sangha's long association with Jeta Vana started this way and they started using the temporary shelters built there by Sudatta. Tathagata held continuous dialogue there with the people of Shravasti.

Soon thereafter, King Prasenjit of Kosala stopped by one day at Jeta Vana to meet Tathagata. The king asked, "*Shramana* Gautama, do you claim to have attained enlightenment as Buddha?"

Tathagata said, "I do claim that."

King Prasenjit said, "In fact, many of the Brahmans and *Shramanas* I know, claim that. How can you claim that considering that you are so young?"

Tathagata said, "Your majesty, there are four things in this world that you do not disregard because they are young: a warrior, a snake, a fire, and a monk."

The king got the message since he was similar in age to Tathagata. He decided to be a lay follower of Tathagata and took the three refuge vows. This was the beginning of a long association between Tathagata and King Prasenjit.

Sudatta built quite a few rain-proof shelters in Jeta Vana over the years. King Prasenjit also built Raja Karama Buddha Vihara next to Jeta Vana. Tathagata had many loyal followers amongst the residents at Shravasti. One of the female followers named Visakha built a Vihara called Purvarama Vihara next to Jeta Vana.

Over the years, Shravasti became the most important center of the Sangha. Tathagata spent twenty-five of his rain retreats in Jeta Vana, the first retreat being almost eleven years after Jeta Vana was gifted to the Sangha. By then, the permanent rain shelters had been built. Seven years after having the first retreat there, Tathagata decided to use Jeta Vana as his permanent seat for rain retreats. Thus, Tathagata had a very long and close association with Jeta Vana and Shravasti.

King Prasenjit came often for advice and solace. Once he came and told Tathagata about his disappointment that his wife Mallika bore him a daughter instead of a son. Tathagata told him about all the good things that the daughters brought to the family. Tathagata also remembers when he came to see him after his favorite wife Mallika died. Tathagata solaced him and reminded him about the transient nature of life.

King Prasenjit was also very fond of good food and often indulged himself and consequently, he was heavy and often not able to enjoy a brisk walk. So, Tathagata had counseled him and his attendants to watch the plate for his good health!

King Prasenjit had become a very good friend over the years. They had so many common areas of interest. They were both closely related in their backgrounds since Kapilvastu was a vassal state of Kosala and owed allegiance to Kosala. The king consulted Tathagata on many of the problems relating to the administration of the state whenever Tathagata was present at Shravasti. King Prasenjit was looking for another wife to marry so that he could have more chances of getting a male descendant. He requested later that a Shakya princess should be offered to him as a bride. After some deliberations, the Shakyas offered Vasabha, daughter of Mahanama who was a cousin of Tathagata. King Prasenjit married Vasabha and, had a son through her called Vidudabha. As the first male child of the king, he was later anointed to succeed King Prasenjit.

As the years passed by, the relationship between the king and Tathagata became deeper and deeper. King Prasenjit provided all the support and security to the Sangha and his friend and guide Tathagata. They also talked about the general problems of life, the small pleasures, and the sorrows, just as any two persons of the same age would!

•••

-18-

Back to Kapilvastu

It was more than two years since Tathagata had visited his father at Kapilvastu. One day he got a message in Rajagriha about the death of his father Raja Suddhodana. He planned to visit Kapilvastu at the earliest to console his bereaved family. He left Rajagriha with a small group of disciples. They first stopped at Vaishali and then proceeded to Kapilvastu and stayed there at Nigrodha Park on the outskirts of the city.

Tathagata met his foster mother Prajapati and Yashodhara at their house. It had been already a few months since the death of his father and all the rituals relating to death had been completed quite some time back. His aunt was feeling quite lonely and devoid of any responsibility, now that his father was there no more to be looked after on a day-to-day basis.

His aunt said, "You, Rahula, and Nanda now live the life of the Sangha. Your father is there no more for me to take care of. I have a proposal for you to consider. Why don't you allow women to enter the Sangha? I would like to join the Sangha along with many women of Kapilvastu who are similarly inclined!"

Tathagata had earlier thought about this matter and

had not allowed women to enter the Sangha because of the many complex issues relating to their security and the need to separate the living arrangements so that sexual desires were avoided. The religious order was still only a few years old and any haste in accepting the women without the proper living arrangements and security would be detrimental to the reputation of the Sangha. So, Tathagata told his aunt Prajapati that he could not accept the women into their religious order. His aunt was disappointed, of course. She raised this proposal again after a few days when she met Tathagata at Nigrodha Park. He had to again tell her in the negative regarding that possibility. She was in tears at his refusal the second time. Tathagata understood her emotions, but as he saw it, he had to stay firm in his decision for the good of the Sangha.

While at Kapilvastu, another serious matter came to Tathagata's attention for the solution of a simmering conflict between the Shakyas and the Koliyas. There was a dam on the river Rohini which demarcated the Shakya republic from the Koliya region. The dam was jointly built earlier by the Shakyas and the Koliyas and they equally shared the water from the dam for irrigation purposes. Because of the shortfall in the rain that year, the water level in the dam had come down significantly to such a low level that it was not sufficient to allow both parties adequate irrigation water. So, there were constant fights and excited nerves between the field workers. A war-like situation had developed between the two neighboring countries. So, he was approached at Kapilavastu to mediate between the parties and to resolve the matter. They thought that since both the countries came under the suzerainty of King Prasenjit of Kosala and Tathagata had good relations with the King, his words would be considered just and would prevail on the occasion.

Tathagata talked with the leading members from both parties regarding their views and then told everyone that a war between the parties would not bring any solution to the problem. Human lives were more important than water for the crops which could be harvested in various ways. Furthermore, the whole problem could go away if the rains came abundantly. Fortunately for both the parties, they agreed with his analysis, and a war was avoided.

Yashodhara came to meet Tathagata at Nigrodha park. She was also somewhat restless like his aunt, now that his father was there no more and there was no need for the routine support required for running a reigning raja's family. She asked Tathagata many questions about Rahula since he was not brought to Kapilvastu as part of this trip, considering the hasty and arduous nature of the trip and his young age. He was left at Rajagriha under the guidance of senior disciples Shari Putra and Maudgalyayana.

Yashodhara changed a lot during the last couple of years. She did not have an iota of any emotional outburst like the last time they met and had fully accepted the challenges of life, as presented moment to moment. To convince Tathagata that she had been transformed over the years into a new persona, Yashodhara gave Tathagata the following poem that she had composed for the occasion:

"Oh Buddha, the lord of my heart,
Life is guided now by your wise words,
I strive towards the goals that you set
For the *Upasikas* of the world.

You brought back the candle of happiness,
That had extinguished at your first departure,
Not knowing how the events would turn out,
For you in the jungles and for us in the palace!

I am toughened from the years of separation,
I am also mellowed from the love,
Tender love by little Rahula,
Love and care from your old parents.

The whole world cheered me to fight,
For the sake of Rahula and me,
To fight against loneliness,
And the pains of unfulfilled love.

Supported your quest for happiness,
Never knowing it to be so harsh,
The cold shivering lonely nights,
And the splashes of hot summers!

Rahula was the hope and consolation,
His babbling talk and smile nourished me!
I alone had to teach him to read and write,
To be brave and sing the song of life!

Rahula too missed a father dear,
Who would take him to the races,
And play with him in the garden,
Or chastise him for naughty pranks!

Overcame the harsh days and nights,
Thinking about where you may be,

Toiling alone half-naked and unfed,
In a deep and sublime trance!

A big relief at your homecoming at last,
That your quest was a great success,
That you preached happiness to the world,
That you were safe and sound in the Sangha.

When you came to see me in our room,
I was so happy to fall at your feet,
And shed tears of relief and happiness,
That you had not forgotten us behind.

You have taken Rahula away from me,
To teach and fulfill your fatherly rights,
That you will make him learned and wise,
But he is missed very much here at home.

I am grateful to be your lay disciple,
Dedicated now to the Buddha and the Dharma,
My days are now spent in deep meditation,
On your teachings and messages to the world.

Now that *Pitasri* is gone from the world,
And we do not provide any royal services,
Completely free am I to offer my services,
To the cause of the Dharma and the Sangha.

Daughters and mothers may be physically weak,
But strong and tough mentally they are,
They are also a great moral force in this world,
 Logical that they become *Bhikshunis* in the Sangha.

This is my sincerest wish, my lord,
That you make me a *Bhikshuni* in the Sangha,
I will then hold the honor of the community,
And dedicate my life to upholding the triple gems!

Tathagata was happy to note that Yashodhara had very well expressed her state of mind throughout the period of her ordeal all these years and that her mood had changed now and she had subtly made the request to be admitted as a *Bhikshuni* in the Sangha. Tathagata told her that he had to brood over that question since there were several critical ramifications to starting a separate *Bhikshuni* Sangha. Yashodhara was disappointed, but decided to wait for a more opportune time!

•••

-19-

Maha Prajapati Gautami

From Kapilvastu Tathagata went to Vaishali on the way to Rajagriha and stayed in the Gabled Hall of Mahavana which was on the outskirts of Vaishali, the capital city of the Lichchavis. While Tathagata was resting, Ananda came and said, "Lord, your aunt Prajapati has come here by walking the whole way from Kapilvastu. She has her head shaven and is wearing yellow robes. There is a whole group of women from Kapilvastu along with Prajapati. Among them is also Yashodhara. They are all with shaven heads and wearing yellow robes. They are looking for direction from you for getting admitted into your order. What do you want me to tell your aunt Prajapati?"

Tathagata said, "Ananda, I had already refused to admit women to the Sangha and I had told as such to the repeated requests of my aunt Prajapati at Nigrodha Park."

Ananda said, "Lord, your aunt Prajapati is a very determined person now and her sincerest wish is to get into the Sangha. See how she has got all this group of women to follow her and walk from Kapilvastu with their blistered feet!"

Tathagata said, "Ananda, I am refusing the entry of the

women because of security reasons and other complexities that would necessitate the operation of the Sangha. I am also concerned that it might jeopardize the future of the Sangha once the women are accepted as members."

Ananda tried to make a case for our aunt Prajapati and asked, "Lord, do you think women in your Sangha can attain perfection?"

Tathagata said, "Yes, they can, Ananda." Ananda said, "If the women are capable of attaining perfection, you must allow them entry for the sake of your aunt Prajapati. She is your aunt and foster mother and raised you with utmost love and care as her child after your mother died!"

At this, Tathagata thought further about the circumstances under which they might be admitted. After considerable deliberations, Tathagata told Ananda that there would be some conditions, which *Bhikshunis* must observe in the Sangha for the sake of their support and safety. Those eight conditions were as follows:

1. A *Bhikshuni* must pay respect to the ordained *Bhikshus*.
2. A *Bhikshuni* must not stay in a nunnery to observe the rains period of three months if there is no *Bhikshu* nearby.
3. A *Bhikshuni* must invite a *Bhikshu* every fortnight to fix the day of *Upasatha* to observe the precepts, meditate, and listen to persuasive talks.
4. A *Bhikshuni* must perform the ceremony of confession by taking the advice of both the *Bhikshu* Sangha and the *Bhikshuni* Sangha.
5. A *Bhikshuni* must observe penance for half a month when she flouts any of the above respect vows.
6. A *Bhikshuni*, after training in the precepts for two

years, has to seek a higher order from both *Bhikshu* Sangha and *Bhikshuni* Sangha.

7. A *Bhikshuni* must not admonish a *Bhikshu*.

8. Having become a *Bhikshuni*, she should be receptive to learning more about Dharma throughout her life.

Ananda quickly memorized the eight conditions, went outside, and repeated the conditions in front of Tathagata's aunt Prajapati. She agreed to all the eight conditions specified by Tathagata, after consulting with Yashodhara and other followers who came along with her to Vaishali.

Ananda informed Tathagata about the acceptance of all the conditions by his aunt. Then Tathagata went outside and welcomed his aunt and foster mother to be the first Bhikshuni. Tathagata himself conducted her ordination as the *Bhikshuni*. Thus, they started the *Bhikshuni* Sangha and his aunt Prajapati became the first *Bhikshuni* of the Sangha. Yashodhara and other ladies from Kapilvastu were also admitted to *Bhikshuni* Sangha thereafter. The senior monks administered their ordination into the Sangha.

Aunt Prajapati was very elated that now she was a *Bhikshuni* in the Sangha and could strive towards her salvation and help others in their endeavors. Besides Tathagata and Rahula, her son Nanda was in the Sangha too, and now she had the honor to pave the way for the women into the Sangha. Her daughter Sundari Nanda also joined the *Bhikshuni* Sangha after some time.

Aunt Prajapati had the distinction of being the most dedicated leader of the *Bhikshuni* Sangha. She became an *Arhat* after a very brief period of training in the Sangha. She was a natural leader and a great soul who was deeply immersed in the spirit of selfless sacrifice. How can Tathagata forget her great sacrifice and love for him when she reared him as her child right after his mother's death on the seventh day of his birth? She was a magnanimous and selfless soul sacrificing her life for the welfare of others and henceforth was called Maha Prajapati. She had to persevere through the hardship of the first few years of establishing the *Bhikshuni* Sangha. Under her leadership, the women of the *Bhikshuni* Sangha were able to maintain the discipline and the rigors of the ascetic living under difficult and ground-breaking conditions. They were able to earn the respect and the support of the men of the *Bhikshu* Sangha and the world at large. For the first time, the world saw a determined group of women striving for their salvation. They proved that they were no less capable to reach for the spiritual heights compared with their male brethren.

Maha Prajapati lived in the *Bhikshuni* Sangha for more than ten years until reaching her Pari nirvana.

To show her depth of dedication and the height of accomplishments as Maha Prajapati Gautami, Tathagata notes here the song that she had written herself in the *Therigatha*, a book of songs, written by the elder *Bhikshunis*:

Oh Buddha, my lord, the greatest being,
You are the brave and the virtuous,
You only removed the suffering from my life,
And the sufferings of other beings like me.

All my sufferings vanished the moment,
I learned the cause – the thirst for things.
I marched on the Eight Great Paths,
To dry up the thirst and the suffering.

Many times, in my births in the *Samsara*,
Came as a mother, son, father, and brother,

Not knowing the things in the proper forms,
Kept on moving without ever getting *Moksha*.

Having had training with the Exalted one,
I know this is my last life in the *Samsara*,
Since my thread of Karma has been weak,
I do not have to take rebirth further.

The disciplined ones achieve their goals,
Every day they carry out severe tasks,
Follow the senior disciples in the Sangha,
Stay content and preach happiness to all.

For the benevolence of the many,
Maya gave birth to Siddhartha,
He saved the people from disease and death,
From the very cause of their pain and suffering.

Pay respects again and again,
For making me the first *Bhikshuni*,
Giving the women a fighting chance,
To prove and excel along with the men.

Let everyone persevere and be happy!
This is the prayer to the Buddha.

●●●

-20-

Yashodhara and Rahula

Yashodhara joined the Bhikshuni Sangha along with aunt Maha Prajapati. That was pre-ordained in the life of Yashodhara! She always supported Tathagata's actions and understood his deep feelings. Tathagata could not have left the house in search of truth without her strong moral support. From the very day he left the house, she had started adopting the life of a *Shramaneri*. So, it was no wonder that in the push to start Bhikshuni Sangha, she was strongly behind his aunt Maha Prajapati at every step of the way. Yashodhara was accepted into the Bhikshuni Sangha right after the entry of his aunt Maha Prajapati.

Yashodhara's joining the Bhikshuni Sangha brought all of Tathagata's immediate family members into the ambit of the Sangha. There was Rahula already in the *Bhikshu* Sangha, still as a *Shramanera* under the guidance of the great Dharma guru Shari Putra. The great Dharma guru Maudgalyayana had taken the responsibility of being the teacher of young Rahula. There were some occasions when Tathagata had the opportunity to teach Rahula a few things regarding life.

During the rainy seasons, they used to live in Jeta Vana near Shravasti. Yashodhara lived in the Bhikshuni

Sangha in her hut amongst the other members. Rahula used to live in the Bhikshu Sangha but occasionally visited his mother in the Bhikshuni Sangha. As per custom, he was not allowed inside the huts assigned to Bhikshunis, but he used to stand outside the hut of his mother and talk with her. So, for the first time, Rahula had the benefits of living together both with his father and mother.

Tathagata especially remembers an occasion when Rahula went to see his mother at her hut and did not see her out on the porch to talk to her. Yashodhara was having pain in her stomach and was lying in her bed. So Rahula asked, "*Mata*, what can I bring you to relieve your pain?" Yashodhara said, "Rahula, my son, in Kapilvastu I used to drink mango juice with sugar to get certain relief. But, how can I ask for specific things during our round of asking alms? We have to eat only what we are given!"

Rahula said, "*Mata*, do not worry, I will get that for you."

Rahula knew that he could get help from his Dharma guru Shari Putra in this connection. So, he went to Shari Putra and stood there with a troubled look on his face. When Shari Putra enquired of him, he said, "My mother is lying in bed suffering from stomach pain." So, Shari Putra asked Rahula, "What do you think would alleviate her pain?"

Rahula said, "I have asked my mother and she said mango juice mixed with sugar would bring relief."

Shari Putra consoled him saying, "Rahula, do not worry. I would make arrangements for that." Shari Putra then talked to King Prasenjit to help in the matter. The King procured mangoes from the grove and personally peeled the covers of the ripe mangoes, squeezed the pulp into a container, and added sugar. He then sent it to Rahula through Shari Putra. Rahula ran to his mother with the container and gave her the mango juice. Yashodhara's pain was very much relieved after drinking the juice.

Rahula grew up in the benign environment of the Sangha and received his lessons regularly from both Shari Putra and Maudgalyayana. But Rahula somehow was in the habit of speaking lies on many occasions. When Tathagata came to learn of that, he wanted to give him a lesson directly in that regard.

Tathagata sent Rahula to a distant town to clear up his mind. Tathagata visited that town after a few weeks. Rahula was overjoyed to see him there. Tathagata ordered him to bring a basin of water and wash his feet. When Rahula finished washing Tathagata's feet, he asked, "Rahula, is this water fit for drinking now?" Rahula replied, "No lord, the water is defiled now."

Tathagata said, "Rahula, let us now consider your case. Though you are my son, the grandson of Raja Suddhodana and a *Shramanera*, who has voluntarily given up everything, you seem to have no control over your tongue and thus you have defiled your mind!"

Once Rahula threw away the water of the vessel, Tathagata further asked him, "Is this vessel fit for holding drinking water now?" Rahula replied, "No Lord, the vessel is dirty now."

Tathagata said, "Rahula, think about your case now. Though you are wearing the yellow robe of a *Shramanera*, are you fit for high purpose now that you have become unclean just like the vessel?"

Thereafter, Tathagata lifted the empty vessel, whirled it around, and asked, "Are you afraid that this vessel may fall and break?"

Rahula replied, "No lord, this vessel is cheap and its loss may not be much".

Thus, Tathagata reminded him, "Think about your case again. You are subject to endless currents of transmigration. Since your body is made of the same substances as other things and will meet the dust too, there is no loss if it is broken. Those who speak untruths are held in contempt by the wise."

Rahula was now filled with shame and Tathagata said to him, "Rahula, if men control their tongues, everything would be fine. The sincere men uphold their love of truth. The man who respects righteousness will endure all the difficulties very faithfully throughout his life."

Rahula was deeply in sorrow now after hearing these words. Tathagata never again had the occasion of getting a complaint on this matter. Rahula sincerely exerted himself to sanctify his life. As a father, Tathagata was extremely happy that he seized the opportunity to teach Rahula these lessons and it worked to uplift his life.

After being in the Sangha for about twelve years, Rahula attained the age of twenty and became ready for ordination. So, he was ordained as a Bhikshu by his Dharma guru Shari Putra during a ceremony at Jeta Vana. Henceforth, Rahula was called Rahula Bhadra by the members of the Sangha. Rahula was sincere and conformed to all the requirements of a monkish life. In a way, Tathagata was sometimes sorry to note that Rahula did not have the opportunity to know any other life except the life within the Sangha. As a father, Tathagata felt that Rahula's lack of experience outside the Sangha perhaps made his personality more focused as a monk. But it had prevented him from gaining the experience Tathagata had of life in Kapilvastu, especially the opportunity to observe and participate in the council. That made Tathagata more mature and realistic about dealing with different kinds of people in various situations. Alas, that was not to be and Rahula had to sacrifice that experience for the sake of staying under Tathagata's guardianship in the Sangha as he grew up.

Tathagata must admit here that the relationship between Rahula and him was very friendly, as it should be between a father and a son. But the relationship between them also was not intimate, since Rahula was always obedient and never expressed any difficulties or problems that he faced. Perhaps, this was because of his training in the Sangha to accept things and not to complain. There were a few occasions when Tathagata tried to help him and bring out more accomplishments from his side. One such occasion was when Tathagata asked him to accompany him on a short excursion to the blind man's forest. A few years had already passed since his ordination and Rahula readily agreed. They went to the forest near Shravasti.

They were sitting together under a tree in the blind man's forest. Tathagata asked Rahula, "Are the eyes, the visible objects, and their consciousness permanent or impermanent?"

Rahula said, "Lord, they are impermanent." Tathagata asked, "How about the ears, the nose, the tongue, the sense of touch, the mind, their respective objects, and their consciousness?" Rahula replied, "Lord, they too are impermanent." Tathagata further asked, "Rahula, is something that is impermanent pleasant or unpleasant?" Rahula replied, "Lord, it is unpleasant." Now Tathagata asked Rahula, "Do you think, it is right to claim something, that is impermanent as own's own?" Rahula replied, "No, Lord." Tathagata further commented, "Rahula, if and when a *Shramanera* understands that, he then avoids the six senses, their sense objects, and the respective sense consciousness. He is not attracted by them anymore and becomes free of passion. Thus, he becomes free of rebirth."

Rahula realized the deep meaning of these comments as Tathagata was speaking and the evil influences regarding rebirth and suffering vanished from his mind. Rahula had become an *Arhat*.

Rahula Bhadra had established a very honorable reputation in the Sangha, as someone who was always committed to the cause of the Dharma and the Sangha. Of course, he was a very obedient son to Tathagata and always helped and cared for Yashodhara as much as he could.

It was perhaps his Karma that Rahula suddenly left them all too soon one day and attained his Pari nirvana. He was visiting a distant area away from Shravasti along with a group of monks. The group was visiting the area to spread the message of the Dharma just after the rainy season.

They got the news that there was an outbreak of cholera in that locality and some monks including Rahula got stricken in the epidemic and passed away. All of them were cremated in that area.

Tathagata was at Jeta Vana when he got the words about Rahula's Pari nirvana. He was very sorry to hear the message. He was so young and so much more he could have done for the world at large, particularly for the Dharma and the Sangha. That was not to be, since the wheels of his Karma stopped. Tathagata was at least consoled by noting that he had already become an Arhat and that this was his last life in the *Samsara*.

Yashodhara was at the *Bhikshuni* quarters in Jeta Vana at the time. Tathagata went to see her right away along with

Ananda. It was just after the sunset. She was sitting outside her hut and saw them coming towards her cottage.

She got a stool from the cottage for him to sit on. Tathagata sat on the stool and Yashodhara sat down on the ground in front of Tathagata. Ananda was standing by near them. Tathagata said to Yashodhara, "I have some bad news to convey to you." Yashodhara anxiously looked at him. Tathagata said, "I just got words that our son is no more! Rahula succumbed to the cholera epidemic along with a few monks in his party."

Streams of tears came out from Yashodhara's eyes. She sat there speechless. There was too much grief inside her heart. There were tears in Tathagata's eyes too. They just sat there looking at the ground without saying any more words to each other. Rahula was the only symbol and the gift of their lives as householders. He was gone now leaving them both parents the memory only of the years with him – from the welcome birth cry to the sudden disappearance!

They shared their grief, silently sitting there. Ananda also sat down in front to console them. It was getting dark now. So, Tathagata got up to get back to his hut. Ananda followed him. Yashodhara went back to her hut silently. They could hear her groaning wail of grief as they started walking away from her hut.

That was a very difficult period for Yashodhara. How could she reconcile the fact that her only child was gone from this world? He was still very young and so much could have happened in his life! Yashodhara was also consoled by the fact that Rahula had become an Arhat and would not be reborn to suffer further. She plunged herself more into the activities of the Sangha and aimed to do more for the young men and women and thus see Rahula in them.

Yashodhara was known by the members of the

Sangha as Bhadra Katyayana and Yashodhara *Theri*. Many referred to her as Rahulamata also. Yashodhara worked very hard to experience and practice the ascetic life and attain her *Moksha*. Through the power of her arduous meditation, Yashodhara attained *Maha Bhiksha*. There were only three other persons who had attained that stage, Shari Putra, Maudgalyayana, and Vakkula Ther, all of them male disciples of Tathagata. She was the only female who had the highest distinction as these other great monks of the time.

Yashodhara stayed at Jeta Vana monastery for most of the rain retreats and led Bhikshuni Sangha until her Pari nirvana at the age of seventy-eight. Just at the time of her Pari nirvana, Tathagata went to see her at her quarters and she said,

"Lord, I am today seventy-eight years old. This is my last birth. Where can I go leaving you? Where is my other shelter? I have already attained nirvana!"

Tathagata agreed with her. She left the world soon thereafter. Thus, ended the story of their love in this life. She was the truest life partner within and outside the bonds of the *Samsara*!

●●●

-21-

King Ajatashatru

King Bimbisara of Magadha always supported the Dharma right from the days of its inception and donated to the Sangha the Venu Vana and the Vulture's Peak. Over the years, King Bimbisara had very cordial relations with Tathagata and the Sangha. Whenever Tathagata came during his many rain retreats at Rajagriha, the King would come to meet him. They always had wide-ranging discussions relating to the administrative affairs of the state and various religious matters. He valued Tathagata's advice and sought that whenever there were problems in his personal or public life. Now, they had both grown old in their respective careers, he a king for almost fifty years and Tathagata a mendicant for more than forty years. Tathagata was only a few years older than King Bimbisara.

It seemed Prince Ajatasatru, King Bimbisar's son with Kosala Devi, the sister of King Prasenjit of Kosala, was now impatient to become the king of Magadha. Tathagata came to learn from Maudgalyayana that Prince Ajatashatru had become close to Devadatta, Tathagata's cousin from Kapilvastu, who had been in the Sangha for quite some time.

In one of Tathagata's meetings with the monks,

Devadatta had publicly requested to pass on the leadership of the Sangha to him since Tathagata was getting too old. Tathagata had rebuked him at the time and had said that no one, not even Shari Putra and Maudgalyayana, could take over the leadership from Tathagata, let alone someone like Devadatta. Because of his evil ways, Tathagata later excommunicated him from the Sangha so that he did not misrepresent the Sangha and harm their interests.

Once he was out of the Sangha, Devadatta tried various schemes to harm the Sangha. Since he knew that King Bimbisara was a very strong supporter and friend of Tathagata, he persuaded Prince Ajatashatru to murder King Bimbisara to become king as soon as possible. The prince entered the bedroom of the king one day and was caught by the guards for having daggers with him. But King Bimbisara pardoned him and said that he would abdicate the throne in his favor if Ajatashatru was so eager to be the king. The old king pardoned the prince for his ill intent. Thus, Ajatashatru became the king of Magadha in 492 BCE.

Ajatashatru's ill intentions against his father did not stop there and he returned cruelty and crude behavior against the love and affection shown by his father. After sitting on the throne for some time, Ajatashatru ordered his father Bimbisara to be imprisoned so that the old king would not be able to interfere or take over the reins. Furthermore, to make things extremely unbearable for Bimbisara, he ordered his people to deprive the old king of proper food and planned to starve him to death that way. He even prevented his mother from visiting his father at the prison. Bimbisara starved to death after some time. Queen Kosala Devi, the mother of Ajatashatru, also died of grief over her husband's death. What a sad twist of events! Tathagata lost a very dear friend and supporter, who always stood by the Sangha from the earliest days.

King Prasenjit, brother of Kosala Devi and King of Kosala, was very much grieved at this turn of events and wanted to give a lesson to his nephew King Ajatashatru. He demanded back the villages near Kashi that were given to the king of Magadha as dowry at the time of the marriage of Kosala Devi with King Bimbisara. When King Presenjit occupied these villages with his troops, King Ajatashatru rushed there with his army and defeated his uncle in the battle. King Prasenjit fled back to his capital Shravasti. There were two more battles between the two and Magadha was victorious on both occasions. In the fourth battle, King Prasenjit cleverly maneuvered the king of Magadha to ambush him and take him as a prisoner along with his elephants. But King Prasenjit was magnanimous in his dealing and pardoned his nephew King Ajatashatru and made peace with him. He gave his daughter in marriage to Ajatashatru and returned villages near Kashi to Magadha. Thus, the young King Ajatashatru got a precious lesson in compassion and magnanimity and saved his own life.

Sometime later, when King Ajatashatru became the father of a son, he understood the real feelings of fatherhood and lamented his ill-conceived and brutal acts against his father. The young king conceded his deep repentance when he met Tathagata one evening at Jeevaka mango grove where Tathagata was staying at the time. That was the only meeting they had between them. Tathagata was happy to see at last that the young king had realized his grievous mistakes of ill-treating his father King Bimbisara, Tathagata's dear friend and disciple.

Tathagata would now tell the story of the other famous disciple at Rajagriha who had donated the Jeevaka mango grove to the Sangha. Tathagata stayed there at the time of meeting King Ajatashatru. Jeevaka was the foremost young physician of Rajagriha and was a disciple of Tathagata. He was the son of a courtesan but was raised by a prince of Rajagriha who had picked him up in an abandoned state after birth. He was raised by the prince and he went to Takshashila, the capital of Gandhara state in the west, to study medicine at the famous university there. When he returned to Rajagriha, he practiced medicine and soon was the royal doctor for Bimbisara. The king had also requested Jeevaka to treat Tathagata whenever there was a need. Jeevaka also provided free services to the members of the Sangha. Jeevaka had become very wealthy from his services as a medical doctor throughout Magadha and the surrounding states. As a loyal supporter of Tathagata, he had donated a mango grove to the Sangha and that was called Jeevaka mango grove. Jeevaka had arranged the meeting of King Ajatashatru with Tathagata at the Jeevaka mango grove to help soothe the guilt feelings that the young king felt sometime after his father's death.

Tathagata's royal friend and disciple King Prasenjit also had a tragic end at the door of King Ajatashatru's entry gate to Rajagriha. Of course, it was not due to any fault on the part of the King of Magadha. While visiting the Shakya state along with his army chief Karayana, King Prasenjit heard about Tathagata's presence at Medalumpa, which was under the administration of Kapilvastu. He wanted to see Tathagata and handed over his royal insignia, the ceremonial sword, and the turban to Karayana waiting outside Tathagata's hut. King Prasenjit walked alone to see Tathagata. They had a long conversation about the fact that they were both old now and of the same age and that the world around was changed along with the new players, his son-in-law King Ajatashatru and Prasenjit's son Prince Vidudabha.

When the King finished his visit with Tathagata and took leave, he found that Karayana had deserted him and had run away with his royal insignia and had left him with a horse and a maidservant only. From there Karayana had gone to Prince Vidudabha and had presented him his allegiance along with the royal insignia. So, Prince Vidudabha marched to the capital Shravasti as the new king of Kosala. When the old king learned of this treachery by Karayana, he decided to go to Rajagriha on horseback and ask his nephew and son-in-law for support against Vidudabha. It was many days of traveling and when he reached Rajagriha, it was late night and the gates were closed. The exhausted old king had to rest in a shed outside the city gate and died early morning from diarrhea and exhaustion. When King Ajatashatru learned of this set of events the next morning, he was very sorry to hear of his uncle's death and performed the last rites in Rajagriha. Thus, the life of another great royal friend of Tathagata ended in a tragedy.

King Prasenjit had been a dear friend and had supported the Sangha immensely. Under his protection, the Sangha had expanded Jeta Vana with various permanent structures for the monks and Shravasti had become the main center of activities of the Sangha. Tathagata was sorry to hear the tragic end of King Prasenjit but was comforted to know that his son-in-law King Ajatashatru had performed the last rites with due regard and honor.

•••

-22-

The Last Days

Tathagata spent the rain retreat in the Jeta Vana at Shravasti in 485 BCE. He had almost spent twenty-five of the rain retreats, each lasting three months, in Shravasti so far. While at Jeta Vana, Tathagata received the news that his senior-most disciple Shari Putra had died near Rajagriha the previous winter due to the illness he suffered. That was a grievous loss for the Sangha. Shari Putra was the one who was the most knowledgeable on the scriptures of the Sangha.

Tathagata started his journey south toward Rajagriha at the end of the rainy season. When he was in the village Ukkavela by the side of the river Ganga on the way to Rajagriha, he heard that his most senior disciple Maudgalyayana died near Rajagriha. Tathagata was especially disturbed to note that he was murdered by hired agents of rival religious schools since he had attracted too many Shramanas from other organizations! The Sangha was poorer because of the death of these two most senior disciples.

Tathagata finally reached Rajagriha and stayed there at Venu Vana. While he was there, minister Vaskara from King Ajatashatru's court met him and asked about his opinion on the possibility of the King defeating the Vrije Federation. Now that King Ajatashatru had firmly established his rule in Magadha, he was looking to expand his empire, and hence the neighboring state was his target.

Tathagata had always admired the Vrije Federation and told the minister that adherence to special seven conditions had ensured the continued prosperity of the Vrije Federation. He had many times told the Vrije council about these conditions and they were:

i. They must meet frequently in great numbers to decide on the problems of the country.

ii. They must agree on the decisions taken and then disperse peacefully to attend to their affairs.

iii. They must not bring into effect new decrees or abolish existing ones, but follow the old constitution.

iv. They must respect and honor their elders and give proper weightage to what they say.

v. They must not misbehave with women and maidens of noble birth and keep them forcibly.

vi. They must honor and respect their shrines and provide them with traditional support.

vii. They must righteously protect and guard the *Arhats* and holy persons.

Tathagata told the minister, "So long as the people in Vrije Federation adhere to these seven conditions, their prosperity is assured."

The minister commented, "If that was so, then I would suggest to the King to create dissensions amongst the Vrije's and divide them up first before the launching of any invasion".

Soon after this meeting, Tathagata left Rajagriha on his way to Vaishali. On the way, they stayed at Pataligrama, on the south side of the river Ganga. The ministers Vaskara and others of King Ajatasatru's courts hosted a lunch for Tathagata at Pataligrama. Tathagata saw the progress being made in the construction of the new capital and the new fortress of Magadha. When Tathagata left the new city to cross the Ganga, the ministers came with Tathagata to bid him farewell and named the gate 'Gautama Ghat' in his honor.

This was already the early summer of 484 BCE when they reached Vaishali. They stayed in the garden of Amrapali, the famous courtesan of the city. She came to welcome them and invited them for lunch the next day and Tathagata accepted her invitation. The Lichhavi community also came and invited Tathagata for lunch, but Tathagata had to refuse them as he had already accepted Amrapali's invitation.

The next day, Amrapali served them a splendid meal in her garden. After the meal, Amrapali took a seat in front of Tathagata and said, "I give this park to the order of monks with Gautama Buddha as the head!"

Tathagata accepted her offer and stayed there for a few days. After that Tathagata went to the village Beluva with Ananda and a few other monks to stay during the rain retreat. He advised most of the Bhikshus to make arrangements to stay around Vaishali during the rain retreat.

During the retreat at the village, Tathagata became severely ill and had great pains in his stomach. He endured somehow the pains suffered and recovered finally. Ananda was very concerned about Tathagata. He said to Tathagata, "Lord, I am very happy to see you up again. Of course, I had the comfort to know that the Lord would never attain Pari nirvana until making arrangements for the Sangha!"

Tathagata was somewhat perturbed at Ananda's remarks implying that Tathagata had not prepared them for his eventual departure from this world. Tathagata said to Ananda, "I have taught everything to the monks without holding back anything on my wrist. I have not appointed anyone as my successor because the Dharma that I have elaborated to the monks is going to be the guide when I am not there anymore. So, you have to seek refuge in the Dharma and yourself as an island of support!"

Tathagata felt better after a few days of further rest and then was able to resume his alms rounds at Vaishali. It was a beautiful feeling to visit the shrines in the city again and just be able to walk around the gardened city.

Tathagata asked Ananda to get all the monks around Vaishali to assemble in the hall. He addressed them one last time and said, "Monks, all sentient beings are subject to decay. I will be attaining Pari nirvana not too long from now. Strive with earnestness!"

They left Vaishali soon afterward to start their journey towards Shravasti. Tathagata knew at that time that he would not see Vaishali again. That was a sad feeling.

They traveled through Bhandagrama, Hathigrama, Ambagrama, Jambugrama, and Bhoganagara and kept on moving in a north-westerly direction. Their goal was to reach Shravasti. While at Bhoganagara, a monk asked Tathagata how to judge the words of a monk who claimed to have heard those particular words from Tathagata's mouth. Tathagata said, "The words of the monk have to be verified against the related words spoken in the sutras and the words from a committee of elder monks selected for the purpose." Tathagata was sure that the monks would keep the words of the sutras alive, although they were not written down. So, the Dharma as spoken by Tathagata in the different sutras would reign as the supreme authority to guide the community of monks and lay followers.

After staying at Bhoganagara for a few days, they moved towards Shravasti. They reached Pava and stayed in the mango grove belonging to Chunda, the silver-smith. When Chunda learned of their arrival in his mango grove, he came and bowed down and sat on the side in front of Tathagata. Tathagata instructed him on the Dharma and told him how to achieve happiness in his life. Chunda invited him and the monks for the lunch next day and Tathagata agreed. Chunda prepared the meal at his place and came the next morning to announce that the meal was ready. They all went to Chunda's place with their bowls. Chunda had prepared a special dish called *Sukara Maddava* (sweetened mushroom curry) and served Tathagata. After eating that Tathagata said, "Chunda, please do not serve this to the monks and bury it in the ground. Only I could digest it."

They left Chunda's place soon afterward. Tathagata felt an attack of dysentery. There were also sharp pains in his limbs. But Tathagata somehow was able to bear them and told Ananda to hasten towards Kusinara.

On the way to Kusinara, Tathagata told Ananda to stop by the wayside. He was feeling sharp pain and was quite weak and thirsty too. So, they stopped and Tathagata asked Ananda for some water. Ananda said that river Kakutha was not very far away and they would get clear water there. But Tathagata persisted and asked for some water. Ananda got some water from a nearby stream and gave it to Tathagata. Tathagata was able to contain his thirst for the time being. At this time, a person from the Malla tribe named Pukkusa stopped by and paid respects to them. He got two new robes and presented them to Tathagata and Ananda. He said he was a follower of Arada Kalama, Tathagata's first teacher at Vaishali.

They continued their march toward Kusinara and soon reached the river Kakutha. Tathagata took a bath in the river and drank some more water and then rested under the mango trees on the other side of the river. After some rest, they continued their journey.

Tathagata finally reached the river Hiranyati and crossed the river along with Ananda and the other monks on the way to Kusinara. But Tathagata was very tired by now and requested Ananda to prepare a place to lie down for further rest on the outskirts of Kusinara.

Ananda prepared a resting area under the Sala trees which were in full bloom at the time. Lying down there under the Sala trees, Tathagata was feeling the sharp pain from dysentery. Tathagata was then convinced that he would not be able to rise again. He told Ananda what to do with his body. He told the monks not to concern themselves with the funeral and let the people of Kusinara take care of it.

Ananda was very dejected and started weeping. Tathagata said to Ananda, "I always said that we had to take leave of our near and dear ones. You have been my constant companion for so many years and have taken care of me with patient kindness. You have gained so much merit! Strive on and soon you will be awakened."

Tathagata laid down there that night under the Sala trees. The next morning when Ananda went for the alms to Kusinara, he told the people in the town about Tathagata's presence and the state of his health. During the day, a few persons from Kusinara came to see Tathagata. Of course, Ananda would not let them disturb Tathagata too much.

There was a *Shramana* Subhadra who came to

visit and Tathagata overheard Ananda driving him out. So, Tathagata asked Ananda to bring him in. Tathagata talked to Subhadra. He requested to get ordained into the Sangha. So, Tathagata instructed Ananda to administer the vows. Subhadra was the last one to be ordained into the Sangha during Tathagata's life.

It was evening time and Tathagata was still resting under the Sala trees. The moon was out in the sky radiating its cool rays. One last time Tathagata told the monks, "I will not be there, but the Dharma that I have taught, and the discipline that we have defined, would be there to guide you all. Be your own master!"

Further, Tathagata asked the monks if they had any questions or doubts in their mind, and that they should request him to answer those now. There was only silence from the monks.

Tathagata finally said, "Forms, feelings, conceptions, volitions, and consciousness which together define the personality are bound to decay. So, monks, strive on and on untiringly!" With these words, Tathagata fell into cosmic silence and reached Maha Pari nirvana. It was the full moon night of Phalguna, the spring month of 483 BCE.

•••

Tathagata in Maha Parinirvana at Kusinara

The Dharma Expands Worldwide

It was not surprising that Maha Kashyapa assumed the leadership of the Sangha after Tathagata's Pari nirvana. He was the most revered monk because he maintained a rigorous ascetic practice while upholding the Dharma. The last rites with the physical body of Tathagata had to wait for a few days until the arrival of Maha Kashyapa at Kusinara. The people of Kusinara came to participate in the last rites along with the prominent leaders from the Malla tribe. The emissaries from the adjoining states came too. After the cremation, the relics associated with Tathagata and the ashes were divided amongst the emissaries from the Shakyas, the Koliyas, the Mallas, the Vrije Federation, Kosala, Magadha, and others.

Maha Kashyapa called for a conclave of all the monks to discuss and formalize all that Tathagata had taught so that the Dharma could give the right uniform guidance as per the words spoken by Tathagata. This First Buddhist Council was held at Rajagriha during the next *Varsha* period under the chairmanship of Maha Kashyapa. Ananda recited all the sutras that he had heard as spoken by Tathagata and these were verified with other assembled monks and then corrected and orally recorded. Similarly, Upali recited the

Vinaya rules and the antecedents associated with each of them and these were verified and noted. The Council also noted down many of the discussions Tathagata had on the Dharma. All of these were, in a later period, formalized as Sutra Pitaka, Vinaya Pitaka, and Abhidharma Pitaka and together called Tripitaka. This formalization of the sayings of Tathagata gave confidence to all the members of the Sangha regarding the continuity of the Dharma in the physical absence of Tathagata.

Tathagata would now provide here a summary of how the Dharma expanded as streams of myriad Buddhist sects and spread all over the world during the last twenty-five hundred years after his Pari nirvana. This would clarify to the world how the Dharma spread without any coercion whatsoever and never with the help of the sword.

The Dharma further spread to different centers in the Gangetic plains after the gatherings of the First Buddhist Council at Rajagriha. There was support for the Sangha from the kings and the ruling classes. In addition to earlier centers at Rajagriha, Varanasi, Vaishali, Shravasti, and Kaushambi, new centers sprung up at Pataliputra (the new capital of Magadha), Mathura, Ujjain, etc.

The Dharma got divided and multiplied over the years into tens of different Buddhist sects in various countries of the world. That happened due to the need to satisfy the diversity of personal and community desires of the people. The Dharma flows like a giant river that divides into tens of different streams before meeting the sea.

One hundred years after the Pari nirvana of Tathagata, there were already sixteen different schools for the teachings of the Dharma. This happened because the different groups interpreted the words of Tathagata in various ways to suit their views. Around this time the Second Buddhist Council was held at Vaishali because there were disagreements between two groups regarding the Vinaya disciplinary rules applicable to different monastics. The group of elders calling for more strict additional rules was defeated in the council and got separated from the main group. This group called itself Sthaviravada or Theravada. Monks of Kaushambi and Avanti formed the nucleus of this sect and their most important center was at Ujjain.

The monks opposing the additional rules during the Second Buddhist Council were called Mahasanghikas. They were in support of more liberal and newer interpretations of Tathagata's words. There arose other groups who wanted non-traditional interpretations of the oral scriptures. After a few hundred years, all of these groups combined with the Mahasanghikas and called their path Mahayana or Greater Vehicle. They believed in the liberation of the whole world and not just the individual. They also associated Tathagata with supernatural powers and added divine entities called Bodhisattvas who were each endowed with special powers.

During Magadha Emperor Asoka's reign in the third century BCE, he adopted Theravada as the state religion and spread the Dharma throughout the territory under his reign, stretching from Afghanistan in the west to Anga in the east, Kashmir in the north to Kalinga in the south.

Emperor Ashoka also spread the Dharma outside of India on a very large scale. He sent his son Mahendra and daughter Sanghamitra to Sri Lanka to spread the Dharma there. Since then, Sri Lanka has been a very important center for Theravada. Soon thereafter, the oral scriptures of Theravada were rendered into written scriptures in Pali. That had helped Sri Lanka in spreading Theravada to Myanmar, Thailand, Laos, and Cambodia. The seafaring provinces of Kalinga, Andhra, and the Tamil-speaking areas on the east coast of India played important roles too in spreading Buddhism to Southeast Asian countries. In these countries, Theravada is still the dominant religious sect today. Theravada also spread to China, Vietnam, and Japan, although it is a minor religious sect in these countries today.

There were Theravada groups in the Sangha who believed in the persistence of a soul-like entity that moved from one existence to another depending upon one's Karma. They believed in the existence of a *Pudgala* in addition to the five *Skandhas*. This belief was called Pudgalavada and these groups were very popular all over India, especially during the reign of King Harsa Vardhana in the seventh century CE.

There arose a few Dharma streams closely resembling Theravada, but different in certain other aspects. Sarvastivada was one such very popular school for almost one thousand years, starting from Emperor Asoka's time. Sarvastivadins believed in '*Sarvam Asti*' or everything exists: past, present, and future exist simultaneously, though they may be in latent stages. During the Third Buddhist Council held at Pataliputra under the leadership of Mogaliputta Tissa, monks believing in Sarvastivada differed from the Theravadins and left the council. They went to Mathura and made Mathura their main center of activities under the leadership of Upagupta. From Mathura, they went to Kashmir and established centers of activities under the leadership of Madhyantika. From Kashmir, Sarvastivada spread to Gandhara, Central Asia, and China. Sarvastivada also spread in all parts of India. In the first and the second century, Emperor Kanishka and his descendants were the most famous royal supporters of this school. The scriptures of this school were written in Sanskrit and many of these scriptures were translated into Chinese. The followers of

Sarvastivada schools believed in the Trikaya philosophy and in that respect, they were akin to the followers of Mahayana.

Dharma Gupta School was a sub-sect of Sarvastivada but had a Vinaya text of its own. It rejected some of the *Pratimoksha* or monastic rules enshrined in the scriptures developed by Sarvastivadins. The Vinaya text of the Dharma Gupta school was translated into Chinese in 152 CE and was being used in all the Far East countries since that time.

Sometime in the first or second century CE, all of the Buddhist groups except the Theravadins called themselves the followers of Mahayana. They believed in the existence of Tathagata in three different forms: Nirmanakaya, Sambhogakaya, and Dharmakaya. They believed that Dharmakaya was the ultimate reality behind all the phenomena in the world. All the sentient beings and things in the world are unified under Dharmakaya and this was akin to the concept of Brahman in Upanishadic thought. Dharmakaya presents itself as Nirmanakaya in the form of the historical Tathagata. Dharmakaya also presents itself as Sambhogakaya in the form of historical Tathagata with all the special marks of excellence and brilliance for teaching the followers of Mahayana.

The followers of Mahayana differentiate themselves as Bodhisattvas, the ones who have the heart of wisdom or *bodhicitta*. Due to their compassion towards the world, they try for the welfare, happiness, and full nirvana of the general public. To get liberation from this world, they look for the greater vehicle or the path. A Bodhisattva stays in this world even after reaching nirvana to help others to steer through the sufferings of the world.

As per Tathagata's teaching, all beings and phenomena are dependent on other beings and phenomena for their arising. In the second century CE, Nagarjuna interpreted this as follows: everything has only conditional existence and does not have any intrinsic existence or permanent self. According to Nagarjuna, everything has neither full existence, nor full non-existence, but they are only between these two states. That is why this was called Middle Way or Madhyamika. According to Madhyamika philosophy, there are two kinds of knowledge: *Samvrati Satya* (conditional truth) which is primarily experienced by people, and *Paramartha Satya* (transcendental truth) which is beyond experience. *Paramartha Satya* is ultimately void and termed *Shunyata* or emptiness because no real person bears this. Nagarjuna's philosophy had a major impact on many of the Mahayana and Vajrayana sects.

Yogacara philosophy was advanced by Asanga and Vasubandhu in the fourth century CE and says that one experiences everything in one's consciousness (*Vijnana*) only, and there is no existence of things outside of the mind. Hence, it is also called 'Mind Only' or *Chittamatra* or Vijnanavada philosophy. The emphasis was on yoga and meditation for controlling the behavior of the mind and hence it was called Yogacara school. As per Yogacara philosophy, *Alay Vijnana* is the repository of all of the personal experiences, and karma-related seeds are stored there. When consciousness adheres to a new life, the remnant of *Alaya Vijnana* is added to that. Yogacara philosophy had a major impact later on Mahayana Zen sects.

Around that time in the first millennium, most of Northern India and Central Asia were predominantly Mahayanist. When Buddhism went to China through the silk route, the ideals of Mahayana appealed to the Chinese. They contributed to the development of new Mahayana sects and the associated scriptures. New Mahayana sutras were developed at this time in India and these sutras were written in Sanskrit. Prajnaparamita Shastra was developed in this period based on Nagarjuna's ideas. Some of the important Mahayana sutras written during this period are the following: Avatamsaka sutra, Saddharma Pundarika sutra, Lankavatara sutra, Hridaya sutra, Sukhavativyuha sutra, Vajrachhedika sutra, etc. A few Mahayana sects germinated in China centered around one or more of these sutras and other factors. These new sects blossomed in China in full force and then were transported from there to Korea. Japan, Vietnam, and other countries. Some of these Chinese Mahayana sects were: Hua-Yen, Tien-Tie, Sukhavati, and Chan.

Hua-Yen is based on Avatamsaka or Flower Garland sutra and concepts from Madhyamika and Yogacara philosophies. It envisages an interdependent and interwoven world, where 'one is all' and 'all is one'. This implies that there is no independent existence of self. This school prospered in the sixth to the eighth century in China and spread to Japan, Korea, and Vietnam from there. Hua-yen school is known as Kegon school in Japan and Todai-ji temple in Nara represents this faith today.

Tien -Tie school started in the sixth century CE and is based upon Saddharmapundarika (Lotus) sutra, where Trikaya philosophy is explained along with an emphasis on faith in Amitabha Buddha. This was one of the first schools that spread to Japan and is known there as the Tendai school. The head temples of these sects are located in Mt. Hiei outside of Kyoto.

In the thirteenth century, Japanese monk Nichiren told his followers that mere repeating of 'Namumyohorenge-kyo' or 'Salutation to the real truth of Lotus sutra' can bring out the Buddha nature latent in everyone. Nichiren Shu is the main sect established by Nichiren. Kempon Hokke Shu sect was started in the fourteenth century by a follower of Nichiren. Nichiren Shoshu is the new sect started in the twentieth century for the common practitioners. There are no priests to officiate during religious functions in Nichiren Shoshu. More recently, Soka Gakkai sect was founded in 1930 CE as a mass movement based upon the veneration of Nichiren and the Lotus sutra. It has spread all over the Americas and Europe besides East Asia.

Sukhavati or Pure Land school is based upon Sukhavativyuha sutra and started in China. It was taken to Japan in the twelfth century and is followed in Japan by Jodo Shu and Jodo Shinshu sects. Adherents flock to these sects because they provide the easiest path towards future birth in the Pure Land by just reciting and praying to Amida Buddha.

Chan Buddhism was taken to China in the sixth century by Bodhidharma, a mystic monk from South India. It emphasizes Dhyana (Chan in Chinese) to quieten the mind so that one can get a glimpse of reality. Lankavatara sutra was one of the scriptures used by Bodhidharma to teach his disciples. It includes many of the ideas of Yogacara philosophy developed in the fifth century CE by Asanga and Vasubandhu. It further directs one to the inner experience which words cannot communicate. Chan was a dominant Buddhist sect in China for the next five hundred years starting from the seventh century CE.

Chan Buddhism came to Japan in the twelfth century and is known there as Zen. The Rinzai sect of Zen follows the practice developed by Lin Chi school that started in China in the ninth century. There are five thousand temples and three dozen monasteries in Japan for this sect. Rinzai Zen initially came to Japan to train the warrior Samurai class and is more vigorous and austere in its training methods. *Koan* reading is practiced more thoroughly in this sect.

Soto Zen is the other major Zen sect in Japan and there are ten thousand temples of this sect sprinkled all over Japan. The head temple at Yokohama controls all the teaching monasteries and temples, except for the original monastery established by Dogen, who brought Soto Zen to Japan in the thirteenth century. Dogen is respected as the greatest Buddhist philosopher of Japan and has written many books of *Koan*. Both of these Zen sects have influenced Japanese life and culture in major ways.

During the sixth and seventh centuries CE, Vajrayana schools appeared in India. They were all based upon Mahayana ideology, but integrated magical and ritual practices to assist the practitioner to attain sublimation of individuality and for the rise of *bodhicitta*. Vajrayana practice spread to Central Asia, Tibet, China, Japan, Mongolia, and the neighboring countries. Today Vajrayana sects are dominant in Tibet, Mongolia, Nepal, Bhutan, and the Himalayan region in India. There are four Tibetan Vajrayana sects.

Nyingmapa sect is the oldest Vajrayana sect in Tibet and was started in the eighth century CE by Santarakshita and Padmasambhava who went to Tibet at the invitation of the Tibetan Emperor. Padmasambhava was able to dispel the fears of the locals by integrating the Tantric practices with the local rituals and tribal demons. Dzogchen or 'great perfection' is the highest path and the central teaching of Nyingmapa. Dzogchen is an esoteric practice and must be learned from a master. Nyingmapa has a white sangha where ordained masters are not celibate. This is in addition to the traditional red sangha where everyone is celibate. The Mindrolling lineage there supported the tradition of women masters also.

Gelugpa sect was started by the disciples of Tsongkhapa in the fifteenth century CE. It emphasizes Vinaya monastic rules, Bodhisattva path, and Madhyamika philosophy. Tsongkhapa's writings on meditation practice are studied to arouse *bodhicitta*. In the seventeenth century, the Mongol rulers appointed the religious head of Gelugpa as the head of Tibet and conferred the title of Dalai Lama. Since then, Gelugpa had been in the leadership position in Tibet until the communist takeover in 1960 CE.

Kagyupa sect was started in the twelfth century and emphasizes direct transmission from the teacher to the disciple on the practice of Tantric methods and meditation. Naropa, Marpa, Milarepa, and Gampopa are the famous ascetics from this sect.

Sakyapa sect was started in the eleventh century and is based upon the teachings of Indian guru Virupa and emphasizes both sutra and Tantric teachings. It is named after Sakya monastery in Southern Tibet. Sakya Trizin is the hereditary male head of the ruling family.

The world of Buddhism mostly stayed unknown in Europe and the Americas until the early nineteenth century. Buddhism came to light through the writings of British, German, and French writers who had the opportunity to stay in Asian countries for extended periods during the colonial rule of the European powers. Theravada is the first one to be explained to the Western world through the writings of Ryes-Davis, Beal, Thomas, and others. Later on, a few of Buddhist scriptures, both Theravada and Mahayana, appeared in translated form through publications by Max Muller and others. At the World Religion Conference held in Chicago in 1893, Theravada was represented by Anagarika Dharmapala of Sri Lanka, and representing the Mahayana sects was the Zen monk Soyen Shaku, Abbot of Engakuji

Rinzai Zen monastery at Kamakura, Japan. Writings of D.T. Suzuki, a disciple of Soyen Shaku, shed further light on Mahayana sects and Zen. Suzuki's first book 'Outlines of Mahayana Buddhism' was a classic, first published in 1906 CE.

The Western world learned a lot about the different sects of Buddhism during and after the Second World War. Soldiers from Europe and the United States were stationed in Asian countries for long periods and were exposed to various sects of Buddhism. This was especially true for the exposure of the various Mahayana sects in Japan and Korea. The communist takeover of Tibet around 1960 CE led to large-scale emigration of Tibetan Buddhists all over the world. They set up many temples and monasteries in Europe and America and started aggressively to spread the teachings of their specific Vajrayana sects.

A few Japanese, Korean, and Vietnamese Zen monks set up their monasteries in Europe and America to spread Zen Buddhism after the Second World War. Besides, there has been a very high level of immigration from Buddhist countries to Europe and America. These immigrant communities have set up temples and monasteries to serve their members and other local communities. Consequently, all of the Buddhist sects are represented now in Europe and America. Buddhism is the newest expanding religion on both of these continents.

The expansion of the Dharma in the Western world would further germinate new forms and new sects to satisfy the needs of the society in these countries. The evolution of the Dharma is a never-ending process and will go on. But the core principles that bind all the Buddhist sects are still based upon the words spoken by Tathagata more than twenty-five hundred years ago!

●●●

- 24 -

Epilogue

It is more than twenty-five hundred years since Tathagata's Pari nirvana near Kusinara in 483 BCE and the world has changed a lot since then. The Dharma has evolved in various directions and expanded the world over. It seems amazing that Buddhism has survived in this world with about a billion souls practicing the philosophy of myriad different Buddhist sects as elaborated in the last chapter. The day they let the women enter the Sangha in 523 BCE, Tathagata had predicted that it would last only five hundred years instead of a thousand years! The Dharma has gone far ahead of his wildest dreams, especially considering that Buddha Dharma essentially vanished in the land of its birth. Traces of the Dharma were even almost wiped out from Gaya, Sarnath, Kusinara, and Kapilvastu until only a few decades back.

Tathagata believes that the unleashing of scientific know-how in the twentieth century, along with the democratization of the world society has heralded a new age of prosperity for the maximum number of people. However, adequate safeguards need to be developed against barbarism by individuals, groups of people, or nations. Tathagata's seven-point advice to Vrije Federation more than twenty-five hundred years back still holds good for the world order today:

- The world communities should meet frequently and in great numbers, not just a few chosen and powerful nations.
- They should conclude the meetings without any acrimony and attend to the affairs of the respective communities harmoniously as one world, bound together inseparably.
- They should uphold the age-old laws of human society, such as respecting the environment, sharing prosperity between the poor and the wealthy, education and health opportunities for everyone, and the basic human rights to live in dignity.
- They must respect and honor the elders in all societies and always listen to their perspectives.
- They must provide proper opportunities to girls and women, and empower them to build a society together with men. They have to protect them from atrocities and unfair treatment.
- They must honor, revere, and respect the shrines in all communities and provide proper support.
- They must protect and guard the *Arhats*, the preachers, and the guardians of all the Dharmas.

The Vrije Federation could not maintain their republics, because they quarreled between themselves and could not uphold all those ideals. What a beautiful, equitable, and highly moral democratic government structure had they established back then! Tathagata had learned a lot from the experience of the Vrije Federation in establishing the laws he set up in the Sangha. The Vrije and other republics were later wiped out by the aggression of the kingdom of Magadha under King Ajatashatru and his successors. The mighty Magadha empire was finally established, stretching from Afghanistan and covering most of northern and eastern India. Later on, the Maurya emperors of Magadha provided a lot of support to the Sangha and helped in spreading the Dharma all over the world. The Kushana empire under Kanishka and his descendants further established the Dharma in Gandhara and Central Asia. The Gupta dynasty after the Kushans also supported the Dharma. Emperor Harshavardhana in the seventh century CE was the last great king in India to support and spread the Dharma.

Tathagata was especially happy at the rise of half a dozen universities in India that were established under the management of the monasteries in the first millennium CE. Tathagata was happy to note that Shari Putra's work arena Nalanda became the seat of the greatest university of the world at the time and was the center of mathematics, logic, and medicine in addition to the traditionally taught study of languages, scriptures, and philosophy of religious sects.

Of course, Tathagata was grieved to note that these great universities along with all of the Buddhist monasteries were destroyed and the monks were murdered. How sad that there was no protection whatsoever from the pillars of society at the time! Once the monks were gone, the Dharma died a natural death in most of India except in the Himalayan belt, which avoided this wanton destruction because of the inaccessibility of the region.

As a religion focused on compassion and non-violence, Buddhism did not have any of its cadres or any other resources to fight against a ruthless and proselytizing army and depended entirely on the protection of the state. Perhaps, this was a weakness of the Buddhist societies and they could not survive the onslaught of Islamic zealots in present-day Iran, Afghanistan, Pakistan, India, Bangladesh, Indonesia, Malaysia, and other countries in Asia.

Tathagata is very elated to note that many versions of the Dharma germinated and prospered in China to suit the divergent groups of people in that vast land. They co-existed with the teachings of Confucius and Tao by suitably adapting some of their practices into the Dharma. Tathagata wishes that the present communist government would keep open the minds of the Chinese people by lifting restrictions on religious observations. As the Chinese people prosper with the help of the open economic policy of the government, they need more and more avenues for satisfying their spiritual hunger. It is quite remarkable that all the different sects of Buddhism are still present in different forms today in China. The south-western provinces have followers of Theravada similar to the people of Thailand and Myanmar. The North-eastern provinces along with the people of Tibet and Inner Mongolia follow the Vajrayana practice. Chan Buddhism and Pure Land practices are sprinkled all over China.

Tathagata is also pleased to note that all of the Buddhist sects from China spread their teachings to Japan, and in that country, these sects blossomed into even more varieties. Today Japan is perhaps the only country where they still have the living versions of most of the Buddhist schools that germinated in India and China.

It is also very surprising for Tathagata to note that the Samurai warriors in Japan adopted Buddhism as a way of life to sharpen their concentration and skills as warriors, and the Japanese military rulers were able to fend off the invasion by the Mongols!

That Japan sidelined Buddhism after the Meiji restoration in the nineteenth century CE and built up an empire focused on aggression towards neighboring countries, led to the tragic events of the two world wars in the twentieth century. A vanquished Japan rightly had realized and adopted the strategy of peaceful co-existence with a strong national defense rather than offense.

The First and the Second World Wars showed the world the specter of large-scale destruction and the futility of pursuing war and aggression as a tool. It is a very satisfying fact for Tathagata that Buddhism has spread to Europe and the Americas, especially, after the Second World War, as a result of the wide-ranging movement of people between the continents. New forms of Buddhist practices are mushrooming in these countries to suit the needs of the people there.

Tathagata is happy to observe that all three versions of meditation practices (Zen or Chan of the Mahayana, Vipassana of the Theravada, and Mandala meditations of the Tibetan Vajrayana) have been making wider appeals to the peoples of the whole world. This shows that human civilization has advanced to a level where a greater percentage of people want to follow the difficult path of meditation practice towards achieving enlightenment, similar to what Tathagata did twenty-five hundred years back!

Tathagata's most important message to the people of the world now is that life in the family is the very basis of human civilization and they must support this institution from all angles. Perhaps a false impression was made by some people that Buddhism was against strong and deep relationships within the family. That is farthest from the real truth. It was only for the monks to renounce the family relationship so that they could fully focus on their goal of achieving salvation through services to society. For the householder, family is the highest responsibility. The family is bound by the loving relationship between the husband and the wife and this love must be maintained for the health of the family. The children are the greatest gifts to the families and the children must be reared with the greatest care and love by the parents.

Tathagata is often judged harshly as a husband and father for leaving home at a youthful age. But the world should note that Tathagata had a beautiful loving relationship with Yashodhara as his wife for thirteen years. They loved each other too much. Tathagata did what he did with the full consent and support of Yashodhara. She was also the most courageous wife for taking over fully the responsibility of baby Rahula. Of course, Tathagata had ensured that they were both in a supportive loving environment along with his parents. The fact that a great part of Tathagata's extended family of Kapilvastu, including his aunt Maha Prajapati, Yashodhara, Rahula, Aniruddha, Ananda, Nanda, Devadatta, etc. joined the Sangha shows the strong family bonds that he had established and supported. Even after becoming a monk, one has to help the earlier members of the family with equal responsibility as one would help any other person.

Tathagata wishes the Dharma to penetrate and focus more on the life of the householders during the next thousand years. Of course, the celibate monks leading the Dharma provided a very key support all these years from the start of the Sangha. There would have been no Buddhism now if the celibate monks were not there! But the main focus of the Dharma should be the householders now and they are also at least fifty times more in number, compared to the number of monks and priests. So, the third millennium should see equal or more participation and leadership by the householders in the Dharma institutions.

Tathagata must say that Buddhism has to celebrate all aspects of life with more vigor. The Four Noble Truths pointed out the reality of the world of suffering, its causes, and its cessation so that life can be steered towards happiness. One must strive to make every moment of life an opportunity to live life happily. The poor and the downtrodden of the world must be helped by the world community to lift them out of their poverty and misery so that a more equitable and happier world leads to peace and prosperity.

The world community must also ensure that the different voices of the people are not suppressed but are expressed in democratic ways. This democratization is indeed needed in all the different spheres of life. Tathagata tried to do that in the religious sphere, and today you see how so many different Buddhist sects blossomed to satisfy the various needs of the people! Tathagata is happy to note in retrospect that his decision not to choose a particular person as his successor was a good one and that the Dharma as the ultimate guide resulted in the creation of multiple sects because of the diverse backgrounds and the needs of the people.

Tathagata notes with much regret that there is no overall communication and coordination between the different religions of the world. There is no common understanding to respect and accept each other. Consequently, there is much misinformation and mistrust and there is very little being done by religious organizations to curb acrimony and violence perpetrated by certain groups of people and some countries.

Tathagata must also exhort all the people of the world to give high priority to the arts, such as painting, sculpture, dance, plays, literature, architecture, etc. in the new millennium so that the whole society lives and prospers satisfying all the innate desires for creativity. The Dharma equally permeates in the creative activities and celebrates these as the culmination of the human spirit!

The destiny of all the sentient beings on this earth is interlinked together, many times more so today than twenty-five hundred years back, because of the extensive use of technology in every aspect of life. Humans must closely coordinate the issues relating to climate change, resource utilization, and environments within the whole world. The middle path that Tathagata had shown could be followed for the proper utilization and sharing of the resources within the world.

During the last hundred years, human society as a whole has developed military arsenals that can wipe out and destroy large countries and even continents. The top countries in the world in terms of military, economic, and political powers are playing a dangerous game of amassing lethal weapons to defend for future wars. But if there is a future large-scale war like the ones in the twentieth century, human society may be obliterated because of the level of military arsenals piled up. Add to that the prospects of biological and chemical warfare and information network warfare. There is no doubt that the destiny of the human race is interwoven with the state of affairs of each large and small nation. The coronavirus pandemic of 2020 has shown how vulnerable and interdependent the countries of the world are irrespective of economic and political power.

It is time now for the world society to behave as one family. The 'Vasudhaiva Kutumbakam' (the world as one family) slogan persisted in India since ancient times and should be truly accepted by all the countries of the world. It is also essential that outright unlawful behaviors of nations are curtailed so that no single country is allowed absolute veto power in the United Nations. Those with or without veto power must behave in line with the majority wish of the world society if countries representing at least ninety percent of the rest of the world population are in support of a resolution offering benefits to the world society. This is only possible if the top countries wielding the power in the United Nations correct their selfish behavior that only serves short-term interests.

The Security Council could still provide the leadership in formulating critical recommendations to the General Assembly. But all coercive decisions against nations must be taken in the General Assembly representing the whole world. These are the challenges for the present world community!

The Dharma accepted all living beings and plants as part of the one interdependent world. Unfortunately, the large-scale industrialization of the world during the last two hundred years has caused immense damage to the overall environment of the world. The world society must work together to protect the environment and not just focus on short-term material gains!

Extremist elements in some countries have resorted to terrorism in recent times to propagate and accomplish their goals. This is highly condemnable, especially if they are for religious causes. There is no place for violence in religion. It should always be based on love, compassion, and persuasion. The world society and every country must root out this evil. Similarly, there is no place for war between countries and the world society must work in a united way to prevent bloodshed due to wars. The main cause behind all conflicts is the superiority complexes of persons and countries whereby they try to subjugate other people and countries for their selfish goals. The world society must honor and reward persons and countries for their good behavior. The countries resorting to wanton selfish aggressions have to be severely punished through trade embargos implemented by the combined will of the world family. This is not possible until the veto system in the United Nations is relinquished by all the vetoing members and it is replaced by a voting system in the General Assembly requiring agreement from countries representing at least ninety percent of the population of the rest of the world, meaning total world population minus the population of the country under consideration. Crucial decisions taken thus would be almost unanimous and very effective as opposed to the present state of affairs in the United Nations. The present Veto system in the United Nations is unjust and unworkable in the long term since it allows the vetoing members to get away with whatever improper actions they carry out.

The Dharma called for the sublimation of the self so that one could achieve supreme happiness and bliss. The same argument also applies to nations to a large extent. The country that shows the most benevolent behavior towards the other nations, large and small, would be rewarded back with more love and admiration. Consequently, more business would flow back in that direction. Many of the strongest nations forget this economics of benevolence and prosperity!

Tathagata wants to remind the world that all the religions of the world including Buddhism had failed to unite human society. They rather divided the people into warring blocks, each one claiming to be a truer representation of the transcendental powers. When Tathagata started the

Sangha, his primary intention was to show the world a path towards happiness in life. Tathagata never opposed paths advocated by other people. Today also Tathagata would say that religious organizations and sects must work together in the common areas of their interests, such as Yoga, meditation, medicine, nutrition, education, and the most important of them all, peace and harmony in society. An organization of all the religions of the world must be developed to help build the world family and smoothen the wounds of the last two thousand years.

Tathagata must say finally that individual liberty and freedom are the most cherished features of human society and without that individual dignity, all the riches and amenities available become superfluous to one's existence in this world. All governments must protect and respect this inalienable right of the individual. In the long term, material and intellectual prosperity are always ensured in a truly free society!

Let every sentient being be healthy, free, and happy!

●●●

Appendix A
Map of Tathagata's World

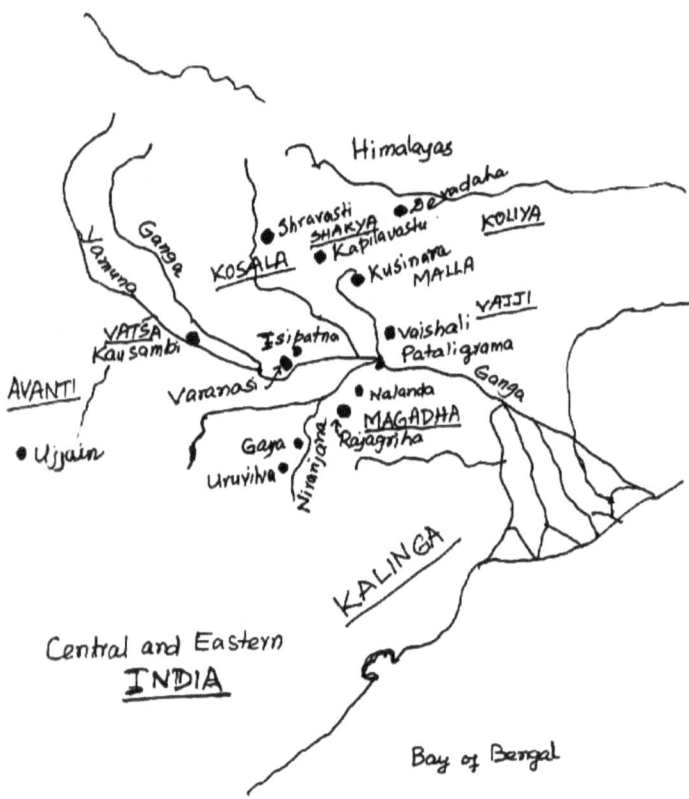

Appendix B
States and their cities, 6th Cent. BCE

Name	Description
MAGADHA	Situated south side of river Ganga, capital at **Rajgriha**, From there, **Nalanda** is on the northern road to **Pataligrama** on the river Ganga, **Gaya** is south on river Niranjana, **Uruvilva** further south on Niranjana.
KOSALA	Situated north of the river Ganga, capital at **Shravasti**
MALLA	Owed allegiance to Kosala state, capital at **Kusinara**
SHAKYA	Owed allegiance to Kosala state, capital at **Kapilvastu**
KOLIYA	Owed allegiance to Kosala state, capital at **Devadaha**
KASHI	Part of Kosala state, capital at **Varanasi**, **Isipatana** is north of Varanasi
VRIJE	Federation Lichchavis, Vrije's and Videhans were the main tribes, capital at **Vaishali**
VATSA	Situated west of Magadha state, capital at **Kaushambi**
AVANTI	Situated further west of Vatsa, capital at **Ujjain**
KALINGA	Situated south of Magadha state

Appendix C
Main Characters and their Relationship

Character	Relation with Buddha
Siddhartha Gautama	The Buddha (Tathagata)
Raja Suddhodana	Father
Queen Maya	Mother
Queen Prajapati (Gautami)	Aunt and foster mother
Yashodhara (Gopa)	Wife
Raja Dandapani	Father-in-law
Queen Amita	Mother-in-law
Rahula	Son
Nanda	Step-brother
Ananda	Cousin brother and disciple
Channa	Charioteer and Attendant
King Bimbisara	King of Magadha and friend
King Ajatashatru	Son of Bimbisara
King Prasenjit	King of Kosala and friend
Prince Vidudabha	Son of Prasenjit
Sudatta (Anathapindika)	Merchant of Shravasti, Disciple
Jeevaka	Physician of Rajagriha, Disciple
Shari Putra	Chief disciple
Maudgalyayana	Senior disciple
Maha Kashyapa	Senior disciple
Devadatta	Cousin brother and disciple
Aswajit	One of the first five disciples
Kaundinya	ditto
Bhadriya	ditto
Vappa	ditto
Mahanama	ditto
Aniruddha	Cousin brother and disciple
Arada Kalama	First meditation teacher in Vaishali
Rudraka Ramaputra	Second teacher near Rajagriha
Vishwamitra	School Teacher at Kapilvastu

Appendix D

Schedule of Main Events in Buddha's Life

563 BCE	Birth of Siddhartha at Lumbini, Kapilvastu
547 BCE	Marriage of Siddhartha with Yashodhara
535 BCE	Birth of Rahula at Kapilvastu
534 BCE	Siddhartha leaves home life
528 BCE	Enlightenment of Siddhartha at Uruvilva
	Dharma-chakra-Parivartan at Sarnath
527BCE	King Bimbisara accepts the Dharma and
	gives Venu Vana to the Sangha
525 BCE	King Prasenjit accepts the Dharma
	at Jeta Vana, Shravasti
523 BCE	Death of Raja Suddhodana at Kapilvastu
508 BCE	Rains retreat for the first time at Jeta Vana
491 BCE	End of reign and death of King Bimbisara
	Ajatashatru becomes the King of Magadha
485 BCE	Death of Yashodhara at Jeta Vana, Shravasti
484 BCE	Death of King Prasenjit at Rajagriha
	The last Rains retreat around Vaishali
483 BCE	Death of the Buddha at Kusinara

Appendix E
Vowel and Consonant Signs

Independent vowel signs, anusvāra and visarga

अ a	आ ā	इ i	ई ī	उ u	ऊ ū
ऋ ṛ	ॠ ṝ	ऌ ḷ			
ए e	ऐ ai	ओ o	औ au		
ṁ	अं aṁ	ः ḥ	अः aḥ		

Virama and dependent vowel signs

क् k	का kā	कि ki	की kī	कु ku	कू kū
कृ kṛ	कृ kṝ	क्लृ kḷ			
के ke	कै kai	को ko	कौ kau		
कं kaṁ	कः kaḥ				

Basic consonant signs

क ka	ख kha	ग ga	घ gha	ङ ṅa
च ca	छ cha	ज ja	झ jha	ञ ña
ट ṭa	ठ ṭha	ड ḍa	ढ ḍha	ण ṇa
त ta	थ tha	द da	ध dha	न na
प pa	फ pha	ब ba	भ bha	म ma
य ya	र ra	ल la	व va	
श śa	ष ṣa	स sa	ह ha	

Appendix F
Complex Consonant Characters

क	क्ख	क्‍क	क्ण	क्त	क्थ	क्र	क्र्य	क्त्व	क्न	क्न्य	क्म
kka	kkha	kca	kṇa	kta	ktya	ktra	ktrya	ktva	kna	knya	kma
क्य	क्र	क्र्य	क्ल	क्व	क्व्य	क्ष	क्ष्म	क्ष्य	क्ष्व	ख्य	ख्र
kya	kra	krya	kla	kva	kvya	kṣa	kṣma	kṣya	kṣva	khya	khra
ग्य	ग्र	ग्र्य	घ्न	घ्न्य	घ्म	घ्य	घ्र	ङ्क	ङ्क्त	ङ्क्त्य	ङ्क्य
gya	gra	grya	ghna	ghnya	ghma	ghya	ghra	ṅka	ṅkta	ṅktya	ṅkya
ङ्क्ष	ङ्क्ष्व	ङ्ख	ङ्ख्य	ङ्ग	ङ्ग्य	ङ्घ	ङ्घ्य	ङ्घ्र	ङ्न	ङ्न	ङ्म
ṅkṣa	ṅkṣva	ṅkha	ṅkhya	ṅga	ṅgya	ṅgha	ṅghya	ṅghra	ṅṅa	ṅna	ṅma
ङ्य	च्च	च्छ	च्छ्व	ज्ञ	च्म	च्य	छ्य	छ	ज	ज्झ	ज्ञ
ṅya	cca	ccha	cchva	cña	cma	cya	chya	chra	ja	jha	jña
ह्य	ज्म	ज्य	ज्र	ज्व	ञ्च	ञ्च्म	ञ्च्य	ञ्छ	ञ्ज	ञ्ज्य	ञ्ज
jñya	jma	jya	jra	jva	ñca	ñcma	ñcya	ñcha	ñja	ñjya	ñja

Appendix G
Main Buddhist Sects Worldwide

Sects	Main Scriptures	Main Countries
Theravada	Vinaya Pitaka in Pali, Sutra Pitaka in Pali, Abhidharma Pitaka in Pali	Sri Lanka, Thailand, Myanmar, Laos, Cambodia
Pudgalavada	ditto	India (sect extinct)
Sarvastivada	Agamas in Sanskrit Dharmagupta Vinaya in Sanskrit	India (sect extinct)
Mahayana	Prajnaparamita Shastra, Mahayana Samutpada Shastra	Asia
Hua-Yen	Avatamsaka sutra	China, Japan (called Kegon)
Tien-Tie	Lotus sutra	China, Japan (called Tendai)
Nichiren Shu	Lotus sutra	Japan
Nichiren Soshu	Lotus sutra	Japan
Soka Gakkai	Lotus sutra	Japan
Pure Land	Sukhavati sutra	China, Japan
Jodo Shu	Sukhavati sutra	Japan
Jodo Shinshu	Sukhavati sutra	Japan
Chan	Lankavatara sutra	China
Soto Zen	Lankavatara sutra	Japan
Rinzai Zen	Lankavatara sutra	Japan
Seon	Lankavatara sutra	Korea
Thien	Lankavatara sutra	Vietnam

Vajrayana	Vajrachhedika sutra	Tibet, Mongolia, Himalayas
Nyingmapa	Vajrachhedika sutra	Tibet
Gelugpa	Vajrachhedika sugtra	Tibet
Kagyupa	Vajrachhedika sutra	Tibet
Sakyapa	Vajrachhedika sutra	Tibet, Nepal
Shingon	Vajrachhedika sutra	Japan

Appendix H
Books for Further Reading

A few books were used as references during the preparation of this book to understand the chronology and details of the historical events and their place in the scriptures. Some of them are listed below:

1. Samuel Beal, *'The Romantic Legend of Sakya Buddha'*
2. H.W. Schumann, *'The Historical Buddha'*
3. Edward J. Thomas, *'The life of Buddha as Legend and History'*
4. E.B. Cowell, *'The Buddha Charita of Ashwaghosha'* (Translation from Sanskrit)
5. Paul Carus, *'The Gospel of Buddha'*
6. E.H. Johnston, *'Ashwaghosha's Buddha Charita'*
7. A.K. Warder, *'Indian Buddhism'*
8. Erich Frauwallner, *'The Philosophy of Buddhism'*
9. Bhikkhu Nanamoli and Bhikkhu Bodhi, 'The Middle Length Discourses of the Buddha: A Translation of the *Majhima Nikaya* (Teachings of the Buddha)'
10. Bhikkhu Bodhi, *'In the Buddha's Words'*
11. Rahul Sankritayana, *'Mahamanav Buddha'* (in Hindi)
12. Shanti Swarup Bouddha, *'Yashodhara'* (in Hindi)
13. Shanti Swarup Bouddha ,*' Mahapajapati Gautami'* (in Hindi)
14. D.T. Suzuki, *'Outlines of Mahayana Buddhism'*
15. Varish Panigrahi, *'Zen Buddhism: Doctrinal Foundations and Practice'*

Glossary

Acharya	teacher, guru
Aham	I or self
Akhada	meeting hall and gymnasium
Anatman	no self, no soul
Anitya	not permanent
Arhat	one who has achieved Nirvana
Ashram	house of a Rishi used for retreat or school
Ashwa	horse
Ashwamedha yajna	horse sacrifice ritual to test sovereignty by powerful rulers
Atman	soul, self
Avatamsaka sutra	flower garland sutra
Avidya	ignorance
Ayurveda	Vedic medical science of life
Arupa dhyana	formless meditation
Bhai	brother
Bhava	becoming, coming to existence
Bhava chakra	wheel of becoming
Bhikshu	Buddhist monk
Bhikshuni	Buddhist nun
Bodhicitta	mind which is filled up with wisdom, the Buddha -nature
Brahman	member of a Hindu priestly caste
Buddha	awakened one
Chakravarty	Emperor of surrounding states
Chan	Chinese for Dhyana, a Buddhist sect in China based on Dhyana
Champak	name of flower with a good smell

Dharma	moral laws in society
Dharma guru	teacher of Dharma
Dhyana	meditation
Dristi	outlook
Duhkha	suffering
Ghat	designated place on the river bank
Henna	name of the flower
Hridaya sutra	heart sutra
Janapada	republic
Jana Pramukh	head of republic
Jataka	birth chart showing planet positions
Jati	birth, a distinct Hindu community
Jaramarana	aging and death
Jhana	dhyana, absorption
Jivika	livelihood
Karma	action, deed
Kshatriya	member of a Hindu warrior caste
Koan	Zen story about a riddle
Lankavatara sutra	sutra spoken at Lanka
Ludo	game of chance
Mahapurusha	great person of wisdom
Mahayana	great Vehicle sects of Buddhism
Mandala	intricate circular drawings used in Vajrayana Buddhism for meditation
Moksha	liberation from the world
Mata	mother
Matasri	honorable mother
Nama-Rupa	name and physical body
Nidana	chain of causation
Nirvana	Buddhist extinction of self
Pahoda	seat on top of the elephant
Pancha Bhuta	five elements
Pari nirvana	final Buddhist extinction when the

	physical body dies
Paramartha Satya	transcendental truth
Parishad	council
Phalguna	first spring month in the lunar calendar
Pipal	large tree with heart-shaped leaves
Pitasri	honorable father
Poornima	full moon day
Prabaja	novice ordination
Pratimoksha	rules of monastic discipline
Pratitya-Samutpada	dependent origination
Prajnaparamita	wisdom excelled
Prayatna	effort
Pudgala	soul-like entity assigned to the person
Raja	king
Rishi	religious learned person
Rupa dhyana	meditation on material or mental objects
Sadayatana	six sense organs and their objects
SaddharmaPundarika sutra	Lotus sutra of good dharma
Sala	big tree that blooms in spring with large scented flowers
Samadhi	state of intense concentration
Samkalpa	solemn resolve
Samsara	existence in the world
Samskara	mental impressions
Samvrati Satya	truth perceived by people, conditional truth
Samyak	right, appropriate
Sangha	Buddhist community
Sankhya	school of philosophy in India
Sanjna	perception, cognition
Sansthagara	assembly hall of the republic

Shramana	mendicant
Shramanera	male mendicant in training
Shramaneri	female mendicant in training
Shunyata	emptiness, voidness, nothingness
Skandha	aggregate of things defining self
Smriti	remembrance
Sparsha	touch
Sukhavativyuha sutra	Pure Land sutra
Swayamvara	choice of the groom by a princess in the open court ceremony
Sesshin	retreat in Zen Buddhism
Tathagata	synonym for Buddha
Thera	elder Buddhist monk
Theravada	sect following original teachings of the Buddha as per Buddhist elders
Theri	elder Buddhist nun
Therigatha	songs of the elder Buddhist nuns
Trilakshana	three characteristics of existence
Trsna	thirst
Upadana	clinging, attachment
Upasaka	a lay Buddhist male
Upasika	a lay Buddhist female
Upasatha	day of observance for cleansing of the defiled mind
Vachana	speech
Vaisakha	first summer month in the lunar calendar in India
Vajrachhedika sutra	Diamond sutra
Vajrayana	diamond vehicle sects, Tibetan and other esoteric Buddhist sects
Varsha	rainy season
Vijnana	consciousness
Viksha	alms

Vipassana	type of meditation followed in Theravada sect
Vedana	feeling, sensation
Yajna	ritual sacrifice
Zen	Japanese for Dhyana, Buddhist sect in Japan based on Dhyana

Black Eagle Books

www.blackeaglebooks.org
info@blackeaglebooks.org

Black Eagle Books, an independent publisher, was founded as a nonprofit organization in April, 2019. It is our mission to connect and engage the Indian diaspora and the world at large with the best of works of world literature published on a collaborative platform, with special emphasis on foregrounding Contemporary Classics and New Writing.